"I tried to avoid this," Axel reminded her.

"I…um." Jennifer wrestled the urge to fling her arms around his neck and kiss him breathless. "Maybe avoidance was a smarter policy than I gave it credit for."

"You called. I came." He stepped closer, backing her neatly into the wall.

She swallowed hard. "Sometimes I don't know what's best for me," she managed to say.

He reached out and skimmed his fingers beneath her hair to encircle the back of her neck, one thumb resting on the pulse point at the base of her throat.

"Axel," she murmured, her sensitive skin registering every callus.

"Mmm?" He never paused the seductive caress.

Jen tried to remind herself of all the reasons she shouldn't be fraternizing with someone she'd be filming. "This may be a bad idea," she warned, her fingers twisting in the fabric of his shirt.

"There's no *maybe* about it." He lowered his head and inhaled a deep breath. "This will only lead to complications."

And then his mouth descended on hers. Axel filled her senses from the minty stroke of his tongue to the silky slide of his lower lip along her mouth. And she realized that bad idea or not, she was in for one wild ride!

Dear Reader,

Hockey players amaze me. Their season is long, their sport can be brutal, and they play multiple games per week—unlike the sweet schedule of the guys over in the NFL. Best of all, you never see them beating their chests and carrying on about their prowess in post-game interviews. They work hard and get the job done without a lot of fuss.

That's one of many reasons I couldn't wait to write about hockey players. I also like the strong camaraderie of hockey clubs who, like baseball teams, spend a lot of time together on the road. There is a real brotherhood forged in that long season.

In the case of Axel Rankin and Kyle Murphy, that brotherhood is even stronger, since Axel was fostered by Kyle's family during his teenage years. With his fierce competitive streak, Axel made a great addition to the Murphy family. And while he'd like to think he's put his past to rest and is ready to move on with his life, the arrival of filmmaker Jennifer Hunter makes that impossible. The trouble is, he can't let her go no matter what the cost....

Happy reading,

Joanne Rock

Joanne Rock

HER MAN ADVANTAGE

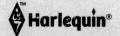

™ **Harlequin**®

TORONTO NEW YORK LONDON
AMSTERDAM PARIS SYDNEY HAMBURG
STOCKHOLM ATHENS TOKYO MILAN MADRID
PRAGUE WARSAW BUDAPEST AUCKLAND

Recycling programs
for this product may
not exist in your area.

ISBN-13: 978-0-373-79688-5

HER MAN ADVANTAGE

www.Harlequin.com

Printed in U.S.A.

ABOUT THE AUTHOR

The mother of three sports-minded sons, Joanne Rock has found her primary occupation to be carting kids to practices and cheering on their athletic prowess at any number of sporting events. In the windows of time between football games, she loves to write and cheer on happily-ever-afters. A three-time RITA® Award nominee, Joanne is the author of more than fifty books for a variety of Harlequin series. She has been an *RT Book Reviews* Career Achievement Award nominee and multiple Reviewers' Choice finalist, including a nomination for *Making a Splash* (Blaze #636) as Best Blaze of 2011. Her work has been reprinted in twenty-six countries and translated into nineteen languages. Over two million copies of her books are in print. For more information on Joanne's books, visit www.joannerock.com.

Books by Joanne Rock

To the readers who take time to write emails,
stop by my blogs and chat with me on Facebook.
You can't imagine how much your words uplift me!
Thank you for your support.

1

"I'm not signing the waiver." Hockey defenseman
Axel Rankin placed the sheet of paper on the desk of
the Philadelphia Phantoms' head coach, Nico Cesare,
hoping like hell his refusal wouldn't be a big deal. He
couldn't be a part of the TV documentary series that
would follow his team over the next month. "There are
enough guys on the team to film. Besides, I'm the defensive goon, not some big headliner."

The native Finn kept the real reason to himself. Axel
couldn't afford to have his personal life broadcast to the
world, the details of his day-to-day in the U.S. available
to old enemies back in Finland. He'd worked too hard to
put that past behind him. Having a camera crew follow
Phantoms players around day and night would only res-
urrect old problems.

"Bowing out is not an option." The coach, a former
goalie and one hell of a leader, passed the waiver back
to Axel, not even looking up from a competing club's
roster filled with margin notes. "The league needs the

publicity and the Phantoms need the exposure. The dictate from corporate is that everyone participates."

Win as a team, lose as a team. Axel had been hearing the same mandate since arriving in Philly on a trade six weeks ago. Cesare's refusal to back off that policy had helped his hockey club earn a spot in the Stanley Cup Playoffs, which would start next week, but that die-hard commitment would make it tough for Axel to cut loose from the group now.

Shit. He ground his teeth, sweat dripping down his forehead from the morning practice session where he'd gone hard from whistle to whistle.

"I've got personal reasons, Coach." He hated to go there. Waving the "it's personal" flag felt like a cop-out.

Cesare finally looked up, his dark eyes meeting Axel's in the austere office decorated with pictures of his two kids and hot, blonde lawyer wife. Other than that, the space was like a computer geek's ode to hockey, full of stats and charts, roster breakdowns of twenty different varieties.

"Then you'll fit right in with the rest of us, Rankin." He tossed his ballpoint onto the desk and threaded his hands together as he rested the palms on his head. "I've got two players who didn't want to sign because they're afraid their wives will get wind of their extracurricular activities on the road from watching the show. I have three guys who don't want their kids referenced in any way, including me. I've got a superstitious player who thinks the cameras will mess up his game rituals. The documentary is shit. I get that. But we're all doing it and we're all signing."

Axel heard the unspoken ultimatum. Sign now or you're not a team player. Or worse—benched.

He hadn't risen up out of a Helsinki ghetto to play on a championship-quality team only to be sidelined now. He'd have to find a way to protect his Stateside foster family from his past if—when—it came calling. Swallowing hard, he picked up the pen his coach had cast aside.

Carefully, he inked his Anglicized name on the appearance waiver, knowing damn well that Axel Rankin wasn't far enough from Akseli Rankinen to fool anyone back home. He was sure his old motorcycle gang kept tabs on him. Waiting for the right moment to call in a favor or blackmail the hell out of him. He figured the only reason they'd waited this long was to ensure his net worth went up along with his newfound success.

"Good man," Nico Cesare assured him, snagging the signed agreement before Axel changed his mind. "You did well in practice this morning. I've got you on the starting line tomorrow night."

Hard-won praise from a notoriously tough critic. Too bad Axel's gut was too full of lead to enjoy the props.

"I won't let you down," he promised, always willing to sacrifice his body to the game. Hockey had helped haul his ass out of the crap life he'd had back home, so he gave it one hundred percent in return.

He just hoped the filmmaking didn't steal his focus, because now he'd have a whole lot more to think about than lofting the Stanley Cup over his head. Stalking toward the exit, Axel planned to head home and make a few inquiries right away. But as he pulled open the heavy glass-and-steel door, his coach called to him.

"Axel?"

Turning, he paused with one foot out in the hall.

"Yeah?"

"The film crew arrived this afternoon." The coach's level gaze gave away nothing. "The director wants to start meeting the team members as soon as possible. You could give it the old stick in the eye and just get it over with. She's set up camp in the conference room."

"She?" Axel tried to weigh what that meant. "We're being followed night and day by a chick?"

He wasn't some backwoods misogynist or anything, but then again, he wasn't a fan of females in the locker room. And hey, to be fair, he wouldn't have taken up journalism and expected free access to the ladies' showers if he was following a women's sport. If he had, maybe he would have been in a whole different career field.

"Her name is Jennifer Hunter. And she looked female to me." The coach grinned, the expression increasing the twist of his nose in a face that could only have belonged to a hockey player. "The good news is, I got the impression she really doesn't want to be here any more than we want a New York filmmaker in our business. So who knows, maybe she'll turn in a lame, half-baked assignment and we'll all get off easy."

It was the first bit of good news Axel had received since hearing about the monthlong documentary special.

"I could do some reconnaissance and see what I can find out. In fact, maybe I could go meet her right now." He'd do it *before* he hit the showers. The smell of unwashed hockey equipment alone could send grown men to their knees. What woman would be able to stand the stench inside an enclosed space like the conference room?

"You're going to make a hell of a first impression, Rankin." Thankfully, the coach didn't seem too upset about that.

Which reaffirmed the message—*win as a team, lose as a team.*

Sometimes, the role of a hockey defenseman was to throw down the gloves and pick the fight to protect his teammates. Axel's responsibility wasn't all that different now. He'd find out a little more about Jennifer Hunter and see why she didn't want to be here. Then he'd make sure she remembered those reasons daily until she packed her camera and left.

That was plan B, and he liked it as a backup. But right now, he'd go with his A game. Charming the socks off the film director by introducing her to the fragrant reality of life in the locker room....

2

"WHERE THE HELL IS THE director lady who's supposed to be in the conference room?"

Filmmaker Jennifer Hunter hid a smile as she eavesdropped on the two-hundred-and-fifty-pound human bullhorn clanging around the hallways of the Phantoms' practice rink in ice skates with a pair of rubber guards on the blades.

The player searching for her had been hammering on the conference room door for two minutes before he started stomping toward the administration offices, his sweaty face glowering. He seemed to have cornered a trainer to demand Jennifer's whereabouts. She—the missing director in question—simply folded her arms on the cold steel railing that circled the practice rink, feeling no great need to identify herself to some self-important player who hadn't even seen fit to pull off his helmet before introducing himself.

Besides, from the ominous tone in the behemoth's voice, she guessed the player wasn't any more enthused about meeting her than she'd been about meeting him. Them. Anyone on the Phantoms' hockey team.

Because, as an activist for social change through her art, Jennifer didn't think affluent athletes were going to make for interesting subjects.

"I'm not sure, Axel," replied the young trainer in matching blue-and-white sweats bearing the team's logo. He flung a clean towel over the player's shoulder and clapped him on the back. "I'll go find out. If you want to hit the showers, I can have an answer by the time you're on the massage table."

Tucked behind a post supporting the high, Plexiglas roof that allowed light to flood the rink, Jennifer wasn't surprised the athletes had celebrity services at their fingertips. It *did* surprise her that the thick-shouldered player wearing jersey number sixty-eight shrugged aside the offer.

"That's okay, Ken," the other man responded, his deep voice matching the fierce expression on his angular face. Thick, dark stubble didn't hide one heavily scarred cheek. His accent made her want to listen to him speak for a long time so she could trace the cadences and vowel sounds. "I'll go ask Nico... Oh, there he is now."

Crap. Jennifer tore her gaze away from the he-man hunky player as the head coach emerged from an office nearby. Not wanting to be drawn out of hiding like a skulking teen since this was an important assignment even if she resented it, Jennifer strode boldly toward the group. She kept her eye on Nico Cesare instead of disgruntled number sixty-eight. The trainer excused himself, leaving her with the looming player and his coach.

"I hope you don't mind that I'm making myself comfortable around the rink, Coach." Smiling, she adjusted a camera strap on her shoulder as if to suggest she'd been busy taking pictures. "You've got an impressive facility here."

As she neared the men, she gained some perspective on their size. Nico Cesare had been seated when she'd been shown into his office, but now he stood beside his player and she could see he'd probably played the game at one time if his height was any indication. The other man—Axel, the trainer had called him—was positively mammoth. Even without the skates he must be at least six-foot-five. His chest was broad enough that she could have lain on him like a bed and had room to roll around.

An odd image considering the moment. Thankfully, she was saved from developing that thought any further as the scent of pungent male sweat assailed her nostrils. The whole rink smelled of hockey equipment, in fact. She'd seen the massive fans in the locker areas that circulated fresh air, but she'd guess no amount of wind power would freshen up a place built on undiluted testosterone.

"I would have given you a tour if I'd known you wanted to see the place right away, Ms. Hunter," the coach returned coolly. "I've got some business to take care of, but at least let me introduce our best defenseman, Akseli Rankinen, a Finnish import we know around here as Axel Rankin. Axel, this is Jennifer unter, who will be a fixture around the team for the next month to film a documentary series."

The coach excused himself, leaving her alone with Axel. Hello, awkward moment. What did a woman do when faced with the man who'd caught her hiding from him? She straightened her shoulders, determined to brazen her way through it. She might not be thrilled about her first commercial project, but if she ever wanted a bigger budget for the meatier social documentaries she enjoyed, she needed to do well here.

"A pleasure to meet you, Jennifer." The defenseman reached for her hand, an odd smile on his face considering he must know she'd been dodging him earlier. He'd seemed so irritated before when he couldn't find her.

But as he leaned in closer for the customary greeting, the sweaty musk of his workout hit her. Damn near choked her.

Then, her eyes watering as she shook his hand, she suddenly understood why he seemed so damn pleased to meet her. His sea-blue gaze twinkled with the sadistic urge to kill her with sweat-stink.

All the more reason not to let him see her flinch.

"The pleasure is all mine, Mr. Rankin," she returned, squeezing his fingers harder in frustration, not that he seemed to notice. He probably had extra muscles there, too. "I've been eager to meet all the players so I can get an idea of potential story lines for the series."

He released her hand in a hurry.

"Story lines?" An unmistakable scowl crossed Axel's

face and she knew a moment's gratitude she wasn't facing this man as an opponent out on the ice.

"Yes. I'll want to see which player is struggling to stay on the team and which one is battling problems at home." She clicked through some of the more basic narratives that came to mind in a piece where ratings mattered. "I'll need to see who will make a good candidate for a love interest—"

"Love interest?" Axel Rankin's color warmed up a shade as his deep voice pitched even lower. The tone was more like a strangled whisper.

And yes, she took a bit of sadistic pleasure of her own in his obvious discomfort since Axel had assaulted her nostrils with deadly intent.

"Yes." She tucked a curl behind her ear, warming up to the job. "Perhaps you have a girlfriend who wouldn't mind a little extra screen time?"

Axel's mouth flattened into a straight line, his face devoid of expression. As if she'd hit a nerve he wouldn't admit. She could be reading into it, of course, but in her field of work she'd gotten adept at coaching nonprofessional actors into evoking a mood on camera. The nuances of body language were well-known to her.

And somehow, she'd upset the hulking defenseman who'd probably sent opponents to the E.R.

"I don't think so, Ms. Hunter." He straightened, his Finnish accent all the more pronounced when he spoke formally. "In fact, I don't think a player's private life should be open for viewing in a documentary that's supposed to be about a sport."

When he moved past her as if to end their conversation, she realized she needed to mend fences. Coming into the Phantoms' rink with a chip on her shoulder about the project had been a bad idea. As frustrated as she might be about this series, she didn't want to alienate all the players before she even began shooting. She had to make a successful series in order to clear the way for what she really wanted to create—a documentary about the way girls used social media to ostracize those they rejected socially. *Bullying* didn't begin to describe how mean-girl culture could stomp out an innocent enemy the way Jennifer's sister, Julia, had been made an outcast by the girls in her school.

And Jennifer had been born with a need to fix problems when she encountered them, a compulsion increased by her single mother's complete lack of parenting. Jen hadn't minded raising herself while her mother worked two jobs and returned to college. But she'd been irritated on her younger sister's behalf when her mother hadn't stepped up for Julia, either. Their father hadn't been a factor, coming around every few years to borrow a few bucks from their mom.

"Of course, you're right." She reached for Axel's forearm. "Some people—believe it or not—jump at the chance to land their friends and family on camera. If you'd rather not, that's fine."

Pausing, he planted his hockey stick on the industrial carpet and seemed to reassess her.

He was a striking man. Not traditionally handsome with that U-shaped scar on his cheek and the stark, angular features softened only by those blue eyes. But the imposing strength of him would give any woman a thrill. Even without the hockey pads, he would be an impressive size.

Her cheeks heated at where her mind went after that, a girly blush that probably hadn't happened to her since high school. And Axel Rankin couldn't have possibly missed it, his eyes roaming over her…lingering here and there for the scenic tour before meeting her gaze again.

"But you'll still be looking for story lines." The blue stare turned darker. Stormier.

And for reasons she couldn't fully fathom, she didn't want to tick him off any more. If only for the sake of the show, she felt called to make nice with him.

"That's part of the job," she admitted. "If all I did was show your team playing hockey, I wouldn't have anything different than a game broadcast. My work will let fans get to know you on a more personal level."

She would find a way to reveal the deeper story behind the game. She'd received critical acclaim in her first two years as a full-fledged director for a small film company. But she had yet to produce anything that made money and her higher-ups insisted she make a more marketable film before she got the green light for the project dear to her heart.

"That wasn't in the job description." He lifted the hockey stick and thudded the end on the carpet once, twice, three times.

"And choking to death in noxious locker rooms wasn't in mine, either, but here I am." She reached for his stick and, leaving it in his hands, she copied his action of tapping it on the floor to punctuate her words. Once, twice, three times. Then she let go. "We might as well make the best of it."

One dark eyebrow lifted.

"Why was a woman who wants to make the best of it hiding from me earlier? Eavesdropping while I wondered aloud where you were?"

"My natural instincts for self-preservation must have kicked in when I heard you banging on the conference room door."

He seemed to consider that, scratching the inside of a shin guard with his hockey stick.

"I might have knocked a bit forcefully," he conceded. "I was anxious to find you before the full effect of my workout died down." He waved a hand around his chest to waft the scent of sweat her way.

Covering her nose with one hand, she used the other to point at him accusingly. "I knew you looked sadistically pleased when you shook my hand. You were trying to asphyxiate me."

He grinned and she was a little surprised to see beautiful, straight, white teeth. Maybe she'd formed a few premature perceptions about hockey players. What other sexy surprises might be hidden inside the six foot five inches of this mysterious man? Suddenly, she was curious to know Axel better.

"Just trying to acclimate you to your new environment." Tugging off his helmet, he unveiled cropped brown hair that was spiked up on top from the headgear. "You'll have to get used to it sooner or later."

Awareness crackled between them even though he didn't seem too happy about it. She wasn't thrilled with the realization, either, but there you go. Who could predict physical chemistry?

"How thoughtful." She found herself eager to see what he looked like after his shower. "Since you're so committed to making me feel welcome, maybe you'd consider showing me around after you wash up?"

She wasn't sure why she'd asked. No, that wasn't true. She knew why she'd asked—she was drawn to Axel Rankin. She'd always struggled with a tendency toward impulsiveness. But she couldn't act on that flash of chemistry when they'd be working together. When she might very well have to extract a story line from him that he wouldn't like.

But it was too late to call back the words.

Surprise registered on Axel's face a split second before heat flared in his eyes.

"They say you should keep your friends close and your enemies closer." He tucked his helmet under his arm. "Guess that means I ought to take you up on the offer."

"Because we're sure to be friends, right?" She needed a few allies on this project if she wanted to get through the upcoming weeks.

He cast her a level glance while the Zamboni made quick work of smoothing over the rink.

"We'll find out soon enough."

AXEL STALLED. BIG-TIME.

He made a few more passes over his chest with the soap, wearing the bar down to nothing after spending so long in the shower willing away his reaction to the mouthy filmmaker. He needed a game plan for sending Jennifer Hunter packing before he did something stupid like act on the surprising attraction.

The woman was seriously hot.

Shutting down the water, he grabbed a towel and dried off, knowing he'd kept her waiting long enough. Frustrated he hadn't figured out how to handle her, he'd have to go with his plan B—learn more about her objections to the film series and exploit those until she wanted to leave.

Except the plan that had made perfect sense in the coach's office two hours ago, didn't sound so good anymore. Especially not since meeting Jennifer had been kind of like taking a puck to the chest—minus the padding.

What was it about her?

Standing at his locker, he pulled on street clothes. Kyle Murphy plowed through the doors while Axel tied his shoes.

Kyle was a forward on the team and also Axel's foster brother. The Murphy family had facilitated Axel's move to the U.S. the summer before his senior year in high school. Kyle and Axel had attended Boston College together before moving to the pros. But while Kyle had been picked up by the Boston NHL team, Axel had bounced around the league before moving to Kyle's team

last fall. Their combined stats had made them appeal-
ing to Nico Cesare as the coach strategized a run at the
Stanley Cup, and he'd signed them as a package deal to
the Phantoms just before the trade deadline.

"Hey, bro." Kyle bumped Axel's fist with his knuckles before moving to his own locker. "Been simmering
in the hot tub?"

"No." He figured shooting the breeze with Kyle was
a legit way to waste a few more minutes before he had
to meet Jennifer again. Hopefully it would be enough
time to get his head on straight. "I'm showing the filmmaker around the facility."

He hadn't been kidding about keeping his enemies
close. If the woman was going to be filming the Phantoms, he wanted to be sure he knew where she was at
all times so he was never caught off guard.

"More power to you, man. You always did go for the
redheads."

Auburn hair was the least of Jennifer's attractions as
far as he was concerned. Sure she had sexy, shoulder-
length red curls. Vivid green eyes. Cute-as-hell freckles and a build so willowy he could probably wrap his
arms around her a few times. But that stuff was window
dressing for the spark inside her, a spark that had flared
from the moment she stepped out from behind the post
to greet him.

She'd been unashamed to eavesdrop, had called him
on his brute behavior without making him feel like a
heel, and then she'd invited him to show her around.
Keeping up with a woman like that would require more

attention than Axel could spare, frankly. But damn. He envied the guy who got the chance to try.

"So you've met her?" Axel tied his shoe, curious what Kyle thought of Jennifer.

"Just a few minutes ago. She was trying to get up into the rafters to see what kind of wide-range camera angles she can snag from overhead."

"You're kidding." Axel slammed the locker shut. "She's here for less than a day and she's climbing the walls?"

"Actually, she was trying to con a janitor into bringing her a ladder."

"Great. She'll probably sue us when she breaks her neck." Tossing his towel in a laundry bin, he jogged toward the door. "Why the hell doesn't Nico assign someone to guard her?"

"Didn't you say you're supposed to be escorting her around?" Kyle called after him. "Sounds like that job lands in your lap, bro."

And wasn't that an image he didn't need in his head?

Axel plowed through the double doors, past the tunnel leading to the ice, toward the viewing area for visitors. At first, he didn't see anyone. The morning session had been closed to the public and most of the players were long gone by now.

He shouldn't have been surprised to hear her voice echo from above his head.

"Up here!" she called, lying prone on a steel girder that was part of the open web truss system holding up the clear glass arena ceiling. She gave a jaunty little wave over her head, her face hidden behind a medium-size camera with a big lens.

"You go to great lengths to hide from me," he observed drily.

"You can't say that when I announced myself right away this time."

"Do you have any idea the kind of insurance liability you pose right now?" How had she gotten up that high? "Weren't you supposed to at least wait for a ladder?"

"Your maintenance staff was concerned about the insurance risk, too. Surprising when you have a doctor and dentist on call for players who break bones every day." The flash from her camera went off and she fiddled with the settings. One red canvas sneaker dangled from fifteen feet up, a hint of ankle visible at the hem of her jeans.

"I'll make sure you have a ladder for the trip down. Can you sit tight while I find one?"

"No need." She stuffed her camera into a nylon bag that hung from her wrist. "The descent is bound to be easier than the climb up."

His heart nearly stopped when he saw her swing down to a lower girder. Positioning himself directly underneath her, he was too busy worrying she'd break her leg to notice the view straight up her colorful Bohemian blouse. Much.

"For someone in the directing business, you sure don't take direction well, do you?" He reached up to spot her, his hand almost touching her leg as she scrambled over the side of the girder.

"Why do you think I stay behind the camera?" Lowering herself with her arms, she hung suspended from the beam, her knees within touching range now.

No one else was around. He'd have to step in and help. Unwilling to risk her falling, Axel wound his arms around her lower legs and squeezed her tight.

"Let go," he ordered, certain he had her. He valiantly did not look up her blouse.

At least not at first… Creamy breasts molded by turquoise lace proved too tempting.

"I don't want to fall on you," she protested, peering down the length of her body at him.

"You won't fall," he assured her, liking the feel of her far too well for a man who intended to send her packing. A man who planned to help her see why this documentary was a very bad idea. "I've got you."

The moment stretched out as they eyed one another and Axel slowly became aware of the scent she wore. The fragrance was subtle and sweet and one he knew well from childhood summers spent in the country.

The fiery redhead smelled like lilies of the valley.

The scent drifted all around him as she let go, giving him her weight. He probably held on to her a second too long, savoring the soft feel of a woman in his arms. With an effort, he tried to recall that the sexy, fragrant female of the turquoise-colored lingerie was an enemy who required monitoring. At the moment, he could only think about how good it was going to feel to lower her body down the length of his.

"Um." She put her hands on his shoulders to steady herself. The camera on a strap at her wrist whacked him in the arm as it followed the movement of her hand. "Axel? Maybe you should…"

She glanced meaningfully at the floor.

He would have preferred to settle her on a bed. A couch. Hell, a futon would be fine with him. But since they were in the middle of the arena seating around the Phantoms' practice rink, he dropped her lightly on her feet, copping only a minimal feel.

How the hell would he chase her away from this film series when he couldn't even keep his hands off her? He needed to reassess his options sometime when he didn't have hints of her scent clinging to his clothes.

"Sorry." He resisted the urge to straighten her blouse where it had ridden up above the waistband of her jeans. "You ready for the nickel tour?"

Her hand smoothed the fabric of her bright purple-and-teal top, covering the sliver of skin he'd spied at her midriff.

"I've been ready and waiting." She gestured expansively to the facility, her cheeks a little flushed. "Show me everything."

Axel had been ducking opportunities left and right, determined to keep this conversation focused on the job she was here to do. But honestly, how could he walk away from that one?

"Tempting as that might be, I think we'd better start with something more manageable." Stalking away from the seats, he gestured for her to follow. "The rink's chiller system, maybe. I'm going to need some cooling down."

3

As THEY PASSED a wall of life-size photos of current Phantoms' players, Jennifer hurried to keep up with her reluctant tour guide. He seemed determined to complete the excursion around the training facility in record time. He'd shown her the state-of-the-art exercise and weight rooms with little commentary, occasionally flipping light switches and nodding to the last few personnel in the building as they went home for the day. Could he make it any clearer that he didn't want to be around her?

His behavior was a puzzle since she knew damn well he was attracted. The heat between them when he'd plucked her from the steel girders had sent her into a full-on meltdown, and she wasn't a woman whose head turned easily. He'd even said he needed a chance to cool down when he finally released her. So he must have been overheated, too.

And resenting it, apparently.

Frustrated with him, with herself and with the way the day was going, she stopped in front of a poster of the team's playmaker, Kyle Murphy. She needed to get to the bottom of this before she moved on. She couldn't scout filming locations for the documentary series until she resolved the Axel dilemma.

"Axel?"

He'd outpaced her by about four miles down the long corridor. Well, at least twenty feet. He turned now, and peered back at her in the semidark vacated part of the building.

"Did I miss something?" His voice echoed a bit in the wide hall with decorative concrete floors polished to a high shine.

"Yes."

She stared him down, willing him to come closer and not be so difficult. For some reason, she felt that if she could win him over to her cause, she could make this film project a success.

"Care to clue me in?" he said finally, not budging.

"Why are you trying to get rid of me?"

Even from twenty feet away, she could see the moment of guilt in his expression. And, while it wasn't necessarily pleasant to have her suspicion confirmed, she appreciated that he had the grace to appear abashed over the fact.

"Am I going too fast?"

"Yes, but that doesn't answer the question. Why are you trying to set a new land speed record?" She wished she had her Nikon in hand now, partially because it felt awkward to ask tough questions with no barrier between her and her subject.

Also because the camera would love this man.

She wanted to linger over the harsh angles of his face with her naked eye. Zoom in on the unusual scar that had to be the outline of a hockey puck under one cheek. Pan out for a long shot of his body to appreciate the way he dwarfed everything around him.

He really did clean up well. His brown hair was shorter than his Viking ancestors', but he had the strong bone structure, which highlighted his magnetic blue eyes. Even without the hockey pads, his physique was extraordinary, a testament to the hours of work in the gym and on the ice. Constant skating, apparently, yielded a truly spectacular butt. She'd been following him around long enough to become familiar with the way the man filled out a pair of jeans.

Now he came toward her slowly, his feet erasing the space between them.

"Maybe I don't like your idea for this movie."

"TV documentary series," she corrected automatically. "I gathered as much when you said that private lives don't belong in a film about a sport."

He paused a foot away from her. Looming.

"So focus on the training. The year-round preparation that goes into playing at this level. Why do you need to manufacture personal lives for athletes who dedicate all their time to hockey?" He leaned closer, as if he could impose his wishes on her through sheer will.

She sucked in a steadying breath and could almost taste the soap he'd used, the warm, clean scent of him filling her lungs and giving her nerve endings a private thrill. Her heart rate tripped into a staccato beat.

"Are you trying to intimidate me?" she asked, her voice little more than a whisper given his proximity and her breathlessness.

"Of course not." He stepped back a bit, though. "Just giving you my opinion. You asked, you know."

"Yes, but when you proclaim it while hovering over me like that, I feel like you're trying to eclipse me with your bigger presence."

"I *am* the team enforcer," he informed her, lowering his brows in a semiconvincing menace while flexing his arms. His chest. Actually, everything seemed to tighten and bulge at once.

"Which means...what? You're going to duke it out with me over this film?" She couldn't help a shiver of awareness at the he-man muscle show, perhaps a leftover genetic reflex from the days when women were driven to seek out strong men for protection's sake.

Because surely she wasn't the kind of woman to be swayed by something so earthy?

"Probably not," he admitted, his expression clearing as his gaze did a slow sweep of her. "But as the Phantoms' newly imported enforcer, my role is to be on the alert for threats to my teammates."

"And you've decided *I'm* the threat?"

"Definitely." His eyes zeroed in on her lips and her mouth went dry.

She shook her head, trying to deny it, but the movement felt slow. Leaden. Almost as if she didn't want to say no to whatever it was they were talking about—she'd forgotten in the hypnotic lure of his proximity.

"Say what you want," Axel said, coming closer again, within easy touching distance. "That look in your eyes right now is threatening the hell out of me. You might not know it, but I'm in big-time fight-or-flight mode this very minute standing next to you."

Any possibility of breathing was gone. She'd probably start hyperventilating at any moment. Beside her, his chest rose and fell as if he was engaged in battle.

"That's ironic," she managed finally, her voice sounding far away and not like her own. "Because I can't seem to move."

His eyes widened a fraction before he narrowed his gaze. That battle he'd been waging? She suspected he'd decided the outcome.

"I tried to outrun you," he reminded her, his voice a soft, minty breath. "You saw me try to avoid this."

The gentle words chipped away at her defenses, surprising her with the note of stark honesty. She hadn't seen where this was headed, but apparently he had.

The thought evaporated along with the rest of her brain waves when Axel stepped even closer, crowding her.

"I...um..." She wrestled with a sudden urge to fling her arms around his neck and kiss him until he was as breathless as she felt. "Maybe avoidance was a smarter policy than I gave it credit for."

"You called. I came." His last step backed her neatly into the wall.

Her heart beat faster. She swallowed hard.

"Sometimes I don't know what's best for me," she managed, her throat dry as she became intensely aware of his chest mere inches from hers.

"That became apparent when you climbed the rafters." He lifted a hand and she held her breath, wondering if he would hold her steady for the kiss she foolishly craved.

Instead, his fingers skimmed beneath her hair to encircle the back of her neck, one thumb resting on the pulse point at the base of her throat. Her neck had never been much of an erogenous zone, but the feel of his thumb softly stroking there struck her as more erotic than full-blown intimate encounters she'd had before.

She wasn't sure if that spoke to how lacking her previous sensual experiences were or what talented hands Axel possessed. Either way, she soaked up the sensation and tried not to arch into him for more.

"Axel," she murmured against the glide of his fingertips along her throat, her sensitive skin registering every callus.

"Mmm?" He never paused the seductive caress.

The rhythm of the touch hypnotized her, making her long to feel it all over her body. How could a simple stroke feel so mind-numbingly good?

Steeling herself, she tried to remember all the reasons she shouldn't be fraternizing with someone she'd be filming. She was a professional, damn it.

"This may be a bad idea," she warned, her fingers twisting in the fabric of his soft cotton button-down.

Sweet, merciful heaven, when had she allowed herself to touch him back?

"There's no maybe about it," he told her, lowering his head and inhaling a deep breath. "This will only lead to complications."

BREATHING IN HER SUBTLE floral scent, Axel told himself to let go of Jennifer.

He needed to pry his fingers off, one by one, and walk away from the insanity. He had her pinned between the wall and the most insistent hard-on of his life, for Chrissakes. This was totally out of line. Unacceptable.

And why the hell couldn't some stray maintenance worker show up right about now to startle them apart? He didn't think anything else—besides a cattle prod— would do the trick.

"I didn't see this coming," she confided, her voice kind of soft and wonder-filled in a way that only wound him up more. "Not for a second."

He kept his head down, eyes on the floor, not ready to see her lips all soft and ready for his kiss. Not ready to see her eyes filled with that hazy, unfocused gaze that meant she was thinking about sex as much as he was.

"No? That's funny because I felt it like a damn freight train headed my way the moment you asked me to show you around."

She stiffened slightly, the subtle shift of her body a movement that inflicted a unique brand of torment on him when he knew this little interlude was going nowhere. At least not today.

"I hope you didn't think I was coming on to you." She managed to sound honest-to-God uptight about it even though her fingers still clutched the placket of his shirt.

"Of course not." He gritted out a semblance of a polite smile as he backed up a step and her hands fell away. "I can see you're not attracted to me in the least."

"Well!" she huffed, crossing her arms in such a way that drew the fabric of her blouse tight across her breasts. "I don't mean that I'm not attracted now. I just meant I wasn't thinking about any such thing back when I asked for the tour."

Following the line of his gaze, she uncrossed her arms. Straightened her blouse. Lifted her chin.

Damn, but he wanted to take her home and tease her some more. Undress her slowly and put that note of awe and wonder back in her voice. But that was not in the plan. He should be chasing her away from the team and most particularly him, not lingering in darkened hall-ways with her.

"Fine. But now you see where this is headed and that it's a bad idea. Can we agree it would be best for all par-ties if the tour ends here?" He needed to regroup some-place else, somewhere far from the scent of lilies of the valley.

He hadn't even seen those damn flowers in over ten years, let alone smelled them. How strange that meet-ing her called up the few rare good memories he had of his childhood home, especially since her project had the potential to bring all the worst ones back to life.

"Agreed." She gave a tight nod. "Thank you for showing me around."

"You're welcome."

He waited for her to storm off in a display of feminine outrage. Stomp down the hall in a huff, maybe. Or sashay away with a little extra hip swing to remind him of what he was missing.

He should have remembered she wasn't a conventional female. She simply frowned, her lips pursed and her brow furrowed. She appeared deep in thought, her gaze focused somewhere above his head.

"Would you like me to walk you to your car?" he prompted in what he considered an inspired moment of chivalrous manners.

His foster mom, Mrs. Murphy, would be proud.

"No, thank you." Her face cleared and she pointed to the wall behind him, where the life-size posters of Phantoms players loomed. "As long as the tour is over, maybe you can tell me a little about your teammates."

And he fought the urge to roll his eyes—he couldn't believe she'd changed gears so quickly when he was still wrestling a massive case of sexual frustration.

"No." He shook his head, needing to be very clear with her. "I can't. Spending time with you is not a good idea for me, whether it's giving you a tour or telling you about the guys. I'm having a career season, Jennifer—"

"Jen. Call me Jen." Not even looking at him, she moved closer to the posters of the players, eyes narrowing to read the text beside Kyle's picture.

"Jen." He angled his body between her and the

write-up, needing to make sure she got the message. "It's important to me to maintain the momentum I've got going while we finish up the regular season. Routine is everything when you're maintaining a streak. I just can't—"

"Am I interfering with your routine?" She peered around as if mystified about what else he'd be doing if not talking to her.

"This whole TV circus is messing up my routine and I only just found out about it." He realized he'd maneuvered close to her again when his body started humming as if he had metal under his skin and she was an industrial-strength magnet.

"Okay, I get it. You want nothing to do with me." Searching around in her purse, she fished out a piece of paper and a pencil. "Can you at least tell me who you would recommend I talk to? Is there anyone on the team who might have a few minutes to spare to give me some insights on the Phantoms?"

Pencil poised, she looked at him expectantly. Here was his out. He could simply give her the name of one of the other guys and someone else could escort her around the rest of the training facility. Their game arena downtown. Someone else could talk to her and catch her when she jumped down from swinging on the girders.

Thinking about how much one of the other guys might like that—and how much he would hate every second of witnessing it—he found he couldn't come up with a name for her.

"How about I call Leandre Archambault?" she prompted, pointing to his teammate's photo on the wall.

Her pencil flew across the paper until he caught it. Halted it. Gripped the damn thing so hard he accidentally snapped it in two. Leandre was the worst ladies' man on the team and he had no intention of letting him anywhere near Jennifer.

"No." He couldn't walk away. Besides, he was better off talking to her behind the scenes, steering her away from him and toward other guys for filming purposes. If she had to film them, Axel would make sure her camera was focused on anyone but him. "I have time to talk to you."

"What about your routine?" One eyebrow quirked, but she didn't seem to be gloating over his inability to cut her loose. If anything, she appeared genuinely interested.

"I'll find a way to make it work." That way he could keep an eye on her. Damn it, he'd known that would be best all along. But the encounter in the hall had rocked him so much he'd second-guessed the plan. "Let's start tomorrow, though. Give us time to regroup."

She nodded.

"Great. And because I appreciate it so much, I'm going to promise you that I will keep my hands to myself at all times." She held up her hands for him to see and wiggled the fingers for good measure. "See? You're safe with me."

His skin reacted as surely as if she'd skimmed that touch along his bare back. His naked abs.

Desire slammed him like a body check to the boards.

"Right." He waved her away from the display toward the conference room so she could gather her stuff. "Too bad it's not you I'm worried about."

4

"IS IT TRUE YOU'RE MAKING a movie about the Phantoms?"

The speaker squatted into Jennifer's vision as she sat in the practice rink's viewing seats at 10:00 a.m. the next morning. While the players ran a slapshot drill out on the ice, Jennifer worked at her laptop, making notes to ask Axel. Well, she *tried* to work on her laptop.

The hopeful young face blinking up at her from the row of seats below prevented her from concentrating. The lithe brunette in a knit beret clutched a paper coffee cup in both hands, hovering over the steam drifting up like a nebulizer while the players lofted puck after puck at their backup goalie.

"Not a movie. A documentary series." Jennifer tried to smile politely, wishing she'd known that today's morning skate was open to the public.

She would have given her cameraman the day off. Bryce's equipment attracted attention and questions.

"I'm Chelsea, groupie extraordinaire." The young

woman thrust out a hand. "Let me know if I can be of any help."

Taking the woman's hand, Jennifer shook it briefly, reassessing.

"A fan?" Her gaze went from Chelsea to the guys on the ice—mainly Axel, whose number she found immediately through the glass boards.

He stood on a blue line—she had discerned the significance of that location last night in a mega cram-session on hockey. Apparently the blue lines marked the offensive zones and as a defenseman, he was often called a "blue liner" since he frequently played there.

Jennifer's interest in and admiration for his role on the ice had increased the more she read until she found herself enthused to return to the rink today. But part of that enthusiasm died at the notion of groupies. Did he have female fans who shadowed his movements? The idea rankled. What if caressing strange women in deserted halls was all in a day's work for a national league hockey player?

"Yes. There are four of us who follow the team whenever possible." Chelsea gestured to a threesome of coffee-clutching young women two rows down. They appeared to be twenty to twenty-five years old. Unlike the stereotype of attention-seeking groupies who dressed to get noticed, this crowd wore appropriate clothes for a hockey rink—jackets and scarves with the blue-and-white team logo. They squealed as two of the players skated their way, giving them a grin and a nod.

"Do you attend a lot of these practices?" Jennifer wondered what kinds of jobs the young supporters had if they could afford to tailor their schedules around a hockey team.

"We come to these all the time, sometimes even when they're not open to the public." Chelsea flipped a long brown curl from one eye, a hint of a tattoo on her wrist visible under her jacket sleeve. "After this, we're headed to Montreal for tomorrow's game. The team flies, but we have to leave earlier since we drive and we want to be there when they touch down."

To do what, exactly? Warm their beds?

Jennifer bit her tongue on the questions, knowing her role here wasn't to judge, or even to get involved. It was simply to document. She had to admit that "not getting involved" part had always been tough for her. When she'd documented poverty, she'd helped educate young moms on wise consumer choices at the grocery store. When she'd made a film on the public school system, she'd found herself volunteering for bake sales. But if the woman in front of her wanted to follow a team of athletes around the country, it certainly wasn't Jen's job to tell her she could do better than that. Although the temptation lingered.

"How interesting." She waved over her cameraman. The stands weren't full for the practice session, so he climbed over the seats to introduce himself to Chelsea before Jennifer explained why she wanted them to meet. "Bryce will be recording a lot of raw footage on this project while we figure out our primary angles for this week's installment. Would you mind if he tagged along on your road trip? Maybe took some footage of your conversations about the team?"

"Really?" Hopping out of her seat, Chelsea sloshed a little coffee out the top of the cup as she waved over her friends. "Almost like we were in the movie, too?"

A whistle blew on the ice and Jennifer noticed the players congregated around the coach.

"You would be." Her attention went back to the woman's wrist where she could have sworn she'd spotted numbers in Phantom blue. An ode to a player? "I'd have to ask you to sign waivers giving us permission to film you and use any footage we obtain, but only a small percentage ever sees the final print."

There was a brief huddled conversation among the women, but it didn't take long for Chelsea to pop out of the cluster.

"We'd love to."

"Great." Jennifer pulled up the waiver page on her laptop and handed Chelsea the stylus so she could sign it electronically while the players seemed to finish up their practice. "Just make sure Bryce knows where to be and at what time to meet you."

While the fans thronged the tunnels off the ice for a chance at slapping hands with the exiting players, Chelsea handed the laptop around to her friends so they could each sign the waiver. When she turned back to Jennifer, her expression had clouded, the initial excitement dimmed.

Second thoughts already?

"Is everything okay?" Jennifer asked, not wanting her documentary stars to be second-guessing themselves yet. Any misgivings had to wait until the series was edited and printed.

Although she knew Axel would have reservations every moment of filming until she returned to New York. She respected his privacy, in theory, even if her assignment here proved at odds with his personal preferences. But was there a deeper reason behind how fiercely he protected his privacy? Most athletes saw the benefit of media attention on their careers, and it turned out Axel Rankin was having a banner year on the ice.

Why so camera shy?

"Sure." Chelsea still held Jennifer's laptop, her eyes fixed on the ice where Axel and Kyle Murphy—his foster brother, she'd learned in her reading—were laughing with the goalie. "I'm glad the documentary will help the team. Maybe boost ticket sales."

"It probably will," Jennifer agreed, trying to see which one of the guys Chelsea had her eye on since all the others had headed to the locker room by now.

She turned back to Jennifer. "But the guys are so great, I almost hate to share them, you know? Kind of like when the newspaper reviews your favorite dive restaurant. Soon everyone's showing up to try the grub and it's not the same anymore."

While Jennifer tried to puzzle through Chelsea's concerns—lack of access to the players, maybe—she reached for her laptop.

And, as Chelsea extended it, her sleeve lifted higher on her wrist. Revealing *#68*, Axel Rankin's jersey number, tattooed on her skin.

THE CAMERAS WERE OUT in full force today.

Axel had noticed as soon as he'd arrived at the practice facility early that morning. Even now, as he waited for Jen to meet him after the team skate, he had to contend with the bright light of a fill flash in his eyes. He'd taken refuge in a practice room to tweak his shot on one of the shooting tarps, but the camera guy had followed him in.

There were three camera operators—all male—who would roam the Phantoms' facilities over the next month. The team had been introduced to the group at the morning meeting. They would attend games and road trips in addition to occasionally following the players home or around town on errands, nights out or anywhere that might be relevant to the larger story. Besides the film crew with handhelds, there were stationary cameras in the rafters above the ice, in the box where players sat between shifts and in a couple of other common areas.

He'd called his foster parents last night to warn them about the documentary. They didn't know the extent of his connections to the motorcycle club back in Finland—ties that hadn't been easily severed. He'd never hidden from the old crew, exactly. He'd known an NHL career gave him a certain amount of visibility, so he'd always been accessible to his enemies. But there'd been a tacit peace these past nine years, with everyone moving on.

Axel wasn't all that sure the peace would hold if this documentary series found a global audience. What would the old gang think of his high-end lifestyle if they saw pictures up close and personal? Would they be able to forgive what they considered the debt of letting him leave if they could see the evidence of his success from the comfort of their living rooms overseas? He didn't want to push his luck.

So he'd told the Murphys to be on their toes if anyone called looking for more information on him. The wealthy Murphy family had resources to increase security at their Cape Cod compound and he'd advised them to do so, claiming a rise in public interest could bring out the occasional nut job. Better to be safe.

As Axel found his shooting rhythm on a tarp, he tried to ignore the hum of the Panasonic recording his every move and wondered if Jennifer had stood him up.

With how gung ho she'd been to quiz him about the Phantoms the day before, he'd figured she would bombard him with questions the second he left the ice. But an hour and a half after practice, he still hadn't seen a sign of her.

Except, of course, in his mind's eye. She'd set up residence there after yesterday's close encounter, insinuating herself in his thoughts and making him edgy for more.

"Have you seen Jennifer around?" Axel asked the young guy shouldering the video equipment, breaking protocol by addressing him directly.

But hey, the less usable footage they had of him, the better.

Shutting off the camera, the tall, skinny dude shifted it aside. "She might be in the parking lot, setting things up for one of the crew to ride with some fans to Montreal."

"Fans?" Surprised and encouraged that she would devote so much film to people who weren't on the team, Axel decided he'd have to give her a rundown on everyone on the Phantoms support staff.

That alone could occupy a camera for a couple of days.

"Groupies, man." The kid—twenty at the oldest—grinned. "Four girls that came to the morning skate. You're living the dream."

Before he could reply, Jennifer strode into the practice room, her cheeks flushed and her hair windblown.

"Yes, congratulations on that, Mr. Rankin." She thumbed through a stack of notes on her clipboard, her hands a flurry of shuffling. "You're a very fortunate man to be so widely admired."

He'd never been in it for the fame. If anything, that made his life more difficult given the enemies he'd made back home.

"Actually, I think I'm fortunate because I get paid to do a job I love." He handed his stick to an attendant, eager to shake off old ghosts and talk to Jennifer away from the whir of rolling film. "Are you ready to go?"

"Very." Pivoting on her heel, she walked out of the practice room.

She wore a blue-and-white Phantoms T-shirt today, a thoughtful endorsement. A floor-length black skirt with big blue flowers billowed around her legs, a skinny silver chain belt dangling from her waist.

She looked great. He liked her colorful, offbeat style. Her energetic walk and enthusiastic hands when she touched him. He liked everything about her a little too well. But sticking close to her throughout the filming might help him avoid being a central figure in any of the footage.

As for the heat between them? He'd have to gamble they'd be able to handle it.

He had to admit Jen seemed to be keeping a professional distance today.

Hell, he wasn't even keeping up with her, now that he thought about it. Was she pulling the same trick he had yesterday, trying to outpace him?

"Where's the fire?" he asked, lengthening his stride as she headed toward the administrative offices. "Why are you in such a hurry?"

"Just trying to be considerate." She shoved open a door to a small office that should have belonged to the staff travel secretary. Apparently the office had been lent to Jennifer while she was here since an assortment of camera bags crammed the floor and a board with a list of shot sequences had been hung behind the desk. "I know you have to travel tonight for tomorrow's game."

He followed her inside, leaving the door open to ensure they wouldn't have too much privacy. It was being alone with her yesterday that had driven him to touch her. Today would be all business.

"Our flight doesn't leave until seven and I'm already packed. I've got plenty of time."

"Well, I need to make a lot of arrangements before then." She turned to face him, her shoulders tense. Still clutching the clipboard like a flotation device for a woman at sea.

"Jen." He stepped closer in spite of himself, sensing a vibe at work that he didn't understand. "Is something wrong?"

"Honestly?" She slammed the clipboard on the desk, sending a few loose papers flying. "I'm a little creeped out to think you have your own personal fan base following you around to all your hotels when you travel."

A strong reaction from a woman he'd only just met. She couldn't be...jealous?

"I think every big-league sports team develops that kind of following," he said carefully.

"Well, I don't see how you can object to a romantic story line for yourself when you've got a groupie with your jersey number tattooed on her like a neon sign."

A prickle of unease started at the base of his neck. As amusing as it might be to think Jennifer would feel any sort of proprietary claim toward him, he couldn't afford to indulge that kind of thought if it led to him having a feature role in her series.

"The fan you're thinking of happens to have *all* the players' numbers tattooed on her."

"You've *seen* them?" Jaw dropping, she pitched her voice lower.

"Hell no." His response was automatic since she made it sound so sordid. "Well, some of them. You need to understand Chelsea and her friends. They hang out around the team a lot, but the guys don't mind because that whole group has had a rough time of it. Chelsea especially."

Outside the office, a couple of the team higher-ups walked by and Axel gave them a wave. The documentary series had brought in all the big brass, who were excited at the idea of more ticket sales in their future.

"What do you mean?" Jen frowned, and for the first time since he'd seen her today, she didn't look quite so tense.

"I mean she has a hell of a story, but it doesn't have anything to do with me. I, on the other hand, don't have a story. Something I've already made damn clear to you."

"Right." She chewed on her lip, an auburn wave snaking forward to land against her cheek as she looked down. "The trouble is, I don't have a romantic story line. I have a team full of hot athletes, and every one of you is either married, in a committed relationship or too married to the game to think about women."

Ha. Did she really believe that he wasn't thinking about her right now? He'd be lucky to have his head in the game by tomorrow with memories of touching her playing over and over in his brain. Even now, he wanted to get closer to see if he could catch that scent of hers that drove him crazy.

"So follow around one of the guys with a girlfriend. Done deal." Why couldn't she film Kyle and Marissa, the matchmaker his brother had fallen for who now occupied all his free time?

"And do I chronicle a happy relationship with no conflict that will put viewers to sleep? Or a relationship on the rocks—and there's no lack of those, according to preliminary research—and really piss off one of your teammates by showcasing his marital problems to the world?"

"Point taken." More than one guy was going through a messy divorce. Some guys' marriages broke up because their wives messed around while the team was out of town.

Then there were the guys who did the messing around themselves. Ax tried to stay out of stuff like that, but he'd seen enough in his short time with the Phantoms to know there were a few team Casanovas.

"So you see my dilemma." Idly, she ran a fingertip up a stack of paperwork piled on one corner of the desk. Behind her, an open laptop flashed her production company's logo for a screen saver.

"I wonder where you got all your research." He was surprised at the twinge of jealousy that spiked for whoever had gotten to fill her in on the team dynamics last night. "I thought I was the go-to guy for the inside information."

"A good journalist never reveals her sources." She raised an eyebrow and crossed her arms.

"Was he as entertaining as me?"

She studied her nails—filed short but painted with blue and purple stripes.

"Let's just say the anonymous party didn't try to scare me off with the scent of sweat and too much testosterone."

"In other words, you missed me." His testosterone levels seemed to stir when drawn into conversation. He might have taken a step closer to her, too, because he caught a hint of her perfume.

"I was still stinging from your rejection, so you can hardly hold it against me if I was driven into someone else's arms." Glancing up from her nails, she gave him a grin that managed to be wicked and innocent at the same time.

And even knowing that she was messing with him didn't stop a surge of possessiveness he had no business feeling.

"Then I hope you're prepared to start naming names before I have to take out my teammates one by one."

"Hmm. I'd hate for you to sacrifice your season to a jealous streak when I got the inside scoop from the head coach's wife."

The ridiculous wave of relief he experienced was a very bad sign. Knowing that she flirted with him only made it tougher to hold back. This time, she was the one sidling closer.

Good thing they'd left the office door open, right? Too bad the hallway outside had been quiet for a while. All the action was down in the players' area where preparations were being made to transport all the team's gear for the road trip.

"Nico Cesare's wife was your source?" He couldn't

resist tracing the cinnamon wave along her cheek, liking the way her eyelashes fluttered a little at his touch. "I'd be curious to know how exactly you ended up in her arms."

"It wasn't easy, but after some girl talk and margaritas at a local bar, I gave her a hug as a thank-you for the lowdown on the team."

Axel cupped her chin. Tilted her face up. He really needed to kiss away that knowing smile. Remind her that he wasn't the only one whose senses were keyed up and ready to fire into hyperdrive.

Except he couldn't do that.

"Yesterday wasn't a rejection," he said instead, his voice gravelly and harsh, revealing too damn much.

Her nod was the smallest of movements, but he felt it in his hand.

"I know," she whispered, her fingertips landing softly on the back of his hand, as if to hold him there.

With all the time in the world to back off, Axel stared, transfixed, at her soft pink mouth. She would taste perfect. Feel perfect.

And soon, that was all he could think about. How damn good she'd feel. How impossible it would be to keep away.

When their lips met, he gave in to the inevitable, knowing that fighting this would be an uphill battle. He had to give some ground or he'd lose his mind. He wanted Jen too badly.

The slide of her lips over his, the gentle press of her

breasts against his chest, created a roar in his ears. A demand in his blood.

He reached for the door, needing to shut out the world for just a minute. Not finding it with a blind swipe, he cocked open one eye enough to orient himself. But as his hand wrapped around the knob to swing the barrier closed, he found a whole lot more than a frosted glass office door.

A handheld-camera operator stood in the hall, the red Record light blinking while the lens trained on them.

5

CAUGHT ON TAPE!

It sounded like a tabloid headline, but it was Jennifer's life thanks to the traitorous cameraman who'd turned the lens on her. Now, skin still tingling from Axel's touch, Jennifer was back in the conference room on-site at the practice rink. After what had happened, she had no choice but to dial in for a teleconference with her boss, hoping like hell she couldn't get fired for a lip-lock with a guy who was supposed to be her film subject.

"I'm sure it will be fine," she told Axel, who'd gone stone-cold silent ever since the incident.

Great. He was cool as ice while she'd seethed like molten lava ever since their kiss.

The only emotion she'd seen from Axel was when he'd ripped the camera out of Steven's hands, of course. Unfortunately, the problem couldn't be solved by tearing film out of the back of the camera since the digital model streamed a live feed accessible to anyone on the crew. The footage all went directly to a live link.

"I never guessed your crew would film *you*." Axel paced around the long conference table where she had set up her laptop and notes. He couldn't seem to sit, though, his body language restless and tense at the same time.

At least he was still speaking to her, right?

"I never thought they would, either. But to be honest, I haven't worked with this particular crew before." She hit the redial button on her laptop when her boss didn't pick up.

Axel stopped pacing.

"Don't tell me this is your first time directing." He pinned her with his gaze, the air between them still crackling with awareness.

"Of course not." She adjusted the angle of her screen and her elbow hit a stack of tentative storyboard ideas. The papers spilled onto the floor in a messy sprawl. So much for trying to stifle her attraction to him. "I just usually tackle social rights subjects, things that demand an artistic approach with a photo crew that specializes in that kind of cinematography. This time, I was assigned a different crew to capture more commercial hooks."

She'd been on this job for two days and she already hated both words—*commercial* and *hook*. Oh, and of course she was utterly distracted by the hot hockey player prowling around the conference room.

"Jennifer?" Her name blared through the tinny-sounding built-in speakers on her laptop.

On the screen, Colin Bennett's face filled the dialogue window, his tie crooked and his shirtsleeves already rolled past his elbows as he hunched over a table in the editing room back at Bennett Film Works. She could identify the room by all the screens filling the space behind his head.

Screens that contained still shots of her kissing Axel. Oh, crap.

"Colin, I can explain," she blurted, wishing she had more business savvy to go with her artistic eye.

"Good work requires no explanation," her boss returned, tugging off the glasses he only wore when editing film or watching dailies. "This is exactly the kind of angle we need to give the piece more human dimension. But I want a signed waiver from you ASAP, granting permission to use the footage."

She bristled while across the room and out of view of the laptop, Axel froze.

"I'm not granting permission." Thank goodness she had this way out. "I have not signed a waiver and I do not grant permission. Colin, I am filming the team, not joining the cast."

"Get real, Jen." Colin frowned at her from his techno-palace in New York. "If you didn't want to join the cast, you shouldn't have stepped into the story. But you did and the footage is perfect."

Axel sank into one of the big leather chairs that surrounded the long oval table. He stared at her across the polished oak veneer, his blue eyes cold and remote. Hard to believe they'd been kissing less than an hour ago.

Although the proof remained in a wrinkle in his shirt where her hand had fisted the fabric. Her fingers itched to smooth it even now.

"Perfect? It was completely accidental and without my knowledge—"

"Which usually makes for the best unscripted television. You know that." Her boss of three years, the man who'd given her a chance to make the kinds of films she wanted right after her apprenticeship as his assistant, glared at her. "Jen, I made it clear this project wasn't going to be another social diatribe that raked in awards and made no money. This is prime time for a mainstream audience and we're using the footage if you expect to remain on the team."

She felt her jaw drop. Her stomach knot. She couldn't lose this job and Colin knew it. Her credentials were showy but not worth much in the filmmaking industry. Who would hire a director who made beautiful documentaries that only found a viewership through the nation's libraries and a few specialty theaters?

Worse, how would she ever make the film about the dangers of social media in youth culture if she didn't pull off this project first?

"If I sign the waiver—" she paused as Axel bolted out of his seat and resumed his restless prowl around the conference room "—what is my role on location? Am I still directing?"

"Absolutely." Perhaps sensing he had her in an impossible position, Colin turned gracious once again, smiling at her as if he hadn't just threatened her job. "You make the decisions for all the other story lines and you can handle your personal life however you wish. But I reserve the right to keep your story as one of the threads in the final mix, which means you're as apt to be filmed as anyone else."

No wonder Colin had handpicked the camera crew to accompany her to Philadelphia. He'd wanted to ensure the commercial angles were covered, giving the film guys carte blanche to record her as she tried to develop the series. But no matter what she thought of her boss's ruthless tactics, she knew when she'd been beaten.

"Fine," she agreed. Or at least, she agreed until she saw Axel's pacing come to an abrupt halt.

Covering the laptop microphone with her hand, she turned the screen away from them both for marginal privacy.

"What else can I do?" she asked the hulking hockey star whose magnetic appeal had gotten her into this mess. "I can't afford to lose this job."

"Are you sure?" He pinned her with a cool blue gaze. "This guy seems like a prick to work for."

Jennifer pressed her hand tighter over the microphone.

"He's a big-time name in indie film and believe it or not, he usually gives me a wide berth creatively."

Axel lifted a brow. "Blackmailing you into a cameo appearance in your own documentary doesn't sound like a wide berth to me."

"He's letting me make a project that means a lot to me if I do this series first."

"More coercion," he muttered.

"No one else is going to let me develop the other project the way I want and it's…important to me."

He looked as if he wanted to say more. Argue the point. But he straightened and rolled his shoulders.

The massive shoulders of a toned athlete. Gulp.

She shook herself free of his allure. Focus, damn it.

"It's your call, obviously." His words were clipped but polite. "But I've got to warn you that I've shot my last scene in this thing. I'll be on the phone the rest of the day doing damage control. From now on, I'm making sure the only images of me in the final cut feature *on-ice* action."

Under her hand, she could hear her boss calling to her through the teleconference screen. She ignored him, hopeful he wouldn't fire her now that they'd cut a deal.

"No more kissing. I get it," she whispered in an aside to Axel as she muffled the microphone on her computer.

She didn't like it, but she agreed restraint was for the best.

"I didn't say anything about no more kissing," Axel clarified. The stern look he gave her made her grin ridiculously. "From now on, I'm only touching you behind locked doors."

"Wicked man." She really should draw better boundaries. But she was starting to see what he'd meant when he'd said the attraction was like a freight train headed their way.

"I mean it."

Her temperature rose just thinking about clandestine

embraces and stolen touches. How could she possibly continue working with him without acting on the draw between them?

"I know." Her voice hitched on a breathy note and she had to clear her throat before she turned the laptop back toward her again. "Let me just finish things up with Colin and then we'll find somewhere to...talk."

Her cheeks heated just thinking about being alone with Axel. She knew it was only a matter of time before the spark between them flared out of control, and she was on a tight deadline for this piece. The documentary series was supposed to air in episodes that were as close to real time as possible, so she needed to edit the first installment as she went to be ready for the Friday air date.

Maybe she could buy a little time before things with her and Axel came to a head. First she needed to edit some film. Downplay the role of the kiss in the first installment that would be aired by week's end. Only then would she have to face the truth of her attraction to him. And only in private. They'd been interrupted before she'd gotten a good taste of him, but that was a problem she could rectify once she was certain they wouldn't be caught on film...again. Whatever happened between them was private and it was bound to burn itself out by the time she wrapped up her documentary series.

"You want to talk?" Axel nodded slowly, his arms folded over his broad chest. "Good. We've got a flight to Montreal to catch. We'll have lots of time for you to tell me all about the film you want to make so badly you're willing to cut a deal with the devil."

IT WAS EASY TO PACK FOR a road trip when you lived out of your car.

Chelsea Durant jogged through the back entrance of the Phantoms' practice rink into the spring sunshine, ahead of schedule to meet her friends and the camera guy—Bryce someone or other—for the ride up to Montreal. Her beater SUV wasn't technically her place of residence anymore since she currently rented an apartment downtown. But the SUV had been her first home after living on the streets for three years on her own. And even though she'd been in an apartment for two years since those days of living out of the vehicle's cargo compartment, she still kept a bag packed in the back in case she needed to hit the road in a hurry.

Old habits died hard.

Spotting her Ford Escape in the parking lot, she stopped short. There was a man next to the SUV, his features shadowed by a hat and the bright noonday sun. But he was big and looming. Scary.

Heartbeat firing into high gear, she turned on her heel.

"Chelsea?"

The deep male voice from behind didn't slow her down as she headed back toward the building. Toward safety.

"Chelsea?" The man called again, a hint of his Minnesota accent drifting through her consciousness. "It's me. Vinny."

Vincent? The rookie right wing who'd gone out of his way to be kind to her since joining the team this fall?

That made sense. No one wanted to attack her in the Phantoms' parking lot. Wherever the team was, she'd always felt safe. Protected by her own crew of hulking bodyguards.

Feeling a little foolish, she slowed. Turned.

He grinned from his spot in the middle of the parking lot, as if he wasn't sure he should follow her. She took a step toward him and that seemed to be the cue he'd been waiting for. He jogged over to her, a beat-up baseball cap jammed on hair still damp from his shower.

A normal woman would have jumped through hoops to talk to him. Vincent Girard was not only a gifted young athlete on the road to a successful NHL career. He was also handsome in a boy-next-door kind of way. His dark blond hair was clean-cut and short, the bristles standing almost straight up on the top of his head like a 1950s crew cut. A crooked smile hinted at an old facial injury where a series of thin scars spread from a white line on his upper lip. His hazel eyes veered the gamut from gray to green with flecks of brown. And yes, she'd watched him closely since she felt an absurd love for Phantoms players.

How could she be a good groupie unless she knew the life story of every last man on the team?

"Sorry," she called as he jogged closer. "I like to practice parking-lot safety and I couldn't see who was under the hat."

He pulled up the brim and twisted the cap around until he resettled it backward on his head. The hat's team logo was one she didn't recognize—green-and-red with a flaming hockey stick. Maybe it had been a school or college team.

"Is that better?" he asked, his white T-shirt and blue nylon shorts the team uniform for lifting and weight-room workouts.

This outfit was clean, though, the cotton still crisp where it clung to broad shoulders. She remembered he was a farm boy, his muscles earned early in life lifting hay bales. That must have been in his bio when he'd joined the team.

"Yes. Thanks." She folded her arms, unsure of herself suddenly.

Her interactions with the team members had become fairly routine, restricted to high fives after good games or practices, although occasionally she went out to team dinners with the players when they were on the road. Her role then was usually to ward off women, a job she was good at since her time on the street had honed her ability to broadcast a serious "don't mess with me" vibe.

What could Vincent want with her now?

"I heard you're headed to Montreal for the game." He waved her back toward her SUV. "I have something to give you for the trip."

Following, she tried not to watch his awesome body in motion. Being a Phantoms fan gave her a certain amount of freedom to dream about the guys on the team, all the while knowing she was safe from any romantic interest on their part. A couple of the guys had tried to hit on her early in her tenure with the Phantoms. But she'd made it clear she was a sports groupie, not a sex groupie.

And they'd been fine with it, glad to have her cheer for them and make the occasional carload of homemade chocolate-chip cookies for them after a road trip. The team thought of her as a sister these days, a fixture in the stands. The one who cheered them on when they were down.

And given her issues with men from her past, that was the nicest role she could imagine for herself.

Relaxing her guard, she honed her fan-girl knowledge. "Am I remembering right that you're from a small town in Minnesota?"

"I grew up on a farm outside of Cloquet. It's not all that far from Duluth in the northeast corner of the state." His long strides required she pick up her pace. At six foot two, he wasn't even the tallest guy on the team, either. He turned to look at her. "Do you all have your passports for the trip across the border tonight?"

"Enhanced licenses." She'd learned that lesson the first time she'd driven all the way to the Canadian border and hadn't been able to get in. "They're cheaper and they're good enough if you're driving over."

Reaching her vehicle in the small lot that was quickly emptying out, Chelsea saw a small box on the hood.

"I remembered you got lost the last time we went to Boston." He picked up the package and handed it to her. "I thought this might help."

A gift? She couldn't believe he remembered she'd taken a wrong turn on the way to that Boston game. An odd little shiver went through her knowing he'd thought about her. Peering down at the box, she couldn't help a startled gasp.

"A GPS?" She read the brand name and saw the long list of fancy features. She'd salivated over these gadgets long enough in the store to recognize a high-end brand. "Wow. I have a navigation app on my phone, but I've been wanting—" Stopping herself, she recalled that she had no business taking gifts from a man. "But I can't accept this."

"Don't think twice about it. I got it for my sister last year and her husband bought her one, too. Then I forgot to take it back to the store for so long I'm stuck with it anyhow." He took the box from her hands and opened it. "If you pop the locks I'll have it hooked up for you by the time Misty gets here."

He nodded toward the back door where her closest friend emerged with the cameraman who would be accompanying their group to Montreal. Chelsea could hardly pretend Vincent posed any kind of threat in her car when her friend and the camera dude were both within shouting distance. Besides, she'd known Vinny since he'd joined the team. His number was even inked in a special place close to her heart since he'd been the first guy on the team to speak to her directly, the first team member to really draw her into the Phantoms' inner circle and make her feel safe.

The Phantoms were the closest thing she had to a family ever since the summer she was seventeen, when she'd walked out of her mother's makeshift tent by the river. She found herself opening the driver's side door for Vincent.

"Well...thank you." The words were scratchy in her throat and they felt weighty as she said them. Not that she wasn't a grateful person. But as a rule, she did not accept gifts. No handouts. No favors.

That way no one could expect anything of her in return. No one could demand something she "owed them," a situation her mother had found herself in far too often. And the way she'd paid back generous men had turned Chelsea's stomach.

"Actually, Vinny—" she started, about to tell him she'd changed her mind. The memories in her head were too visceral. Too disturbing.

"All done." He slid out of the truck, box in hand and the GPS mounted to her windshield. "I'm so glad someone is going to get some use out of it. Drive safe, Chelsea."

He strolled across the parking lot, whistling, leaving her to wonder what had just happened. She couldn't take her eyes off him as he walked away, even when Misty arrived with the camera guy in tow.

"Seriously, Chelsea?" Misty clutched her chest as if she was about to have a heart attack, her gaze following Chelsea's while the cameraman made a second trip back to the building for more video equipment. "Are you making time with one of the players behind my back?" she teased. "Were you talking to Vinny Girard alone out here just now?"

They were the same age and they'd met in a women's

shelter downtown one winter after Misty's father had kicked her out of the house at sixteen—his new wife hadn't wanted her around. But she'd rebounded quickly, finding work at a makeup counter thanks to her natural gregariousness and good looks. With her dark blue-black hair and green eyes, she had a doll-like fragile beauty that belied the powerhouse personality beneath.

"Don't be ridiculous," Chelsea chided, only able to tear her eyes away now that Vincent disappeared inside the building. "He just wanted to be sure we made it to Montreal safely."

It was incredibly thoughtful, really. Even if she was still a little uneasy at the idea of accepting his generous gift.

"What do you mean?" The question barely left her lips when Misty peered inside the open door of the SUV. "Oh, my God. Did he give you that?"

Her friend was already crawling into the driver's seat for a closer look, her curls spiraling out of control in the spring warmth.

"He had an extra one—"

"And it has maps for Canada! Coolness." Misty tapped in an address on the digital keyboard. "I told you he has the hots for you."

"Excuse me?" Chelsea felt something shift inside her. Her stomach dropped the same way it did when she took a high-speed elevator.

Misty pressed another button on the GPS and re-mounted the screen to the windshield.

"He likes you, Chels. I tried to tell you that earlier this season when he invited you to dinner with the team."

"He didn't invite *me*." She vividly recalled the first time Vincent had suggested they join the Phantoms for one of the team meals. "He invited all of us."

"Only because he knows you would have never said yes otherwise." Misty waved to their other friends, Rosa and Keiko, as they stepped into the parking lot along with Bryce, who seemed to be on his second trip carrying equipment.

Chelsea was so stunned by what Misty was suggesting she couldn't seem to move past it, however.

"Vincent Girard plays in the NHL. He's handsome. He's thoughtful. He's rich. The guy could have any woman he wants."

"Really?" Misty gave her a curious look. "He wants you, Chels. I don't care how much he has going for him, I'm betting he'll have his hands full trying to make that work."

Misty knew about her hang-ups. Her reticence with guys no matter how hot they were. Misty started to move toward their friends, but Chelsea tugged her back, confused and wary.

"What are you talking about?" She knew Vincent liked her, but the relationship was more friendly than anything. He looked at her like a sister, trying to make sure she didn't get lost on the way to a strange city or giving her some company for dinner when the team was on the road.

Misty pinched her cheek as if she was an ancient Italian grandmother doting on a child.

"Wake up, Chelsea. You're so gun-shy you can't see when a guy likes you. Can I help it if I feel sorry for Vin when you won't give him a chance to get close?"

Something about Misty's earnest expression made her realize her friend genuinely believed that Vincent liked her. Really liked her. In a way that was more than just friendly.

Around her, Rosa and Keiko arrived with their overnight bags, excited and giggling over some shared joke. Bryce loaded up another camera and a battery pack into the trunk. But the whole scene unfolded through a dense fog for Chelsea.

She felt light-headed. Dizzy. Sounds grew faint. But it wasn't until she went to speak and couldn't force out any words that she realized she was having a full-on panic attack.

All because a guy might like her.

No wonder Misty felt sorry for Vincent. He might have the world by the tail, but clearly the woman he was interested in was a complete basket case.

FIVE HOURS LATER, JENNIFER had finished her call to her boss and smoothed over the rough edges with him. She'd mapped out a few ideas for subplots in the hockey documentary series—subplots she hoped would be interesting enough to keep Colin from focusing too much on her relationship with Axel—which wasn't a relationship at all, but simply an ill-timed kiss.

Or so she wanted Colin to believe.

Scooping up her notes to review on the team plane to Montreal, she emerged from her office. She'd tried tracking down Axel to speak with him privately before their scheduled departure, but he'd been tied up with phone calls of some sort. He'd sounded harried when they'd spoken, and he'd always had another party on the other line. He'd told her back in her office that he'd have to do "damage control" because of his kiss with her.

Apparently, his appearance in the documentary—specifically his appearance kissing her—was going to cause personal trouble for him. Who would care about him kissing her…besides another woman?

Hurrying down the stairs to meet the bus that would take the team and staff to the airport, Jennifer stopped short. What if a publicized kiss with her was going to create trouble with someone else in his life? That would account for the unease she'd heard in his voice when he was on the phone, as well as his need to do damage control. Could he be the kind of two-timer who would kiss one person while another waited for him at home? With dawning horror, she realized she hadn't even asked him if he had a girlfriend. How had she rushed into kissing a guy without learning such basic details?

"Jen?"

Axel appeared out of nowhere. A leather overnight bag slung over his shoulder, he wore a charcoal-gray suit that must have been custom-made given his size. A silvery-blue tie held in place with a gold pin in the shape of a hockey stick made his eyes appear all the more aqua. He bore little resemblance to the sweaty, fiery competitor she'd met the day before. Now he looked like he would have been at home in Monaco, sidling up to the bar next to James Bond.

In other words, he looked like the kind of man who probably had women falling all over him.

"Did you finish your damage control?" she asked, tipping her chin up and blowing right by him toward the doors that led to the parking area. "I remember you said the on-screen kiss was going to create some problems for you."

He caught up to her easily, her stride no match for his.

"I should talk to you about that," he confided, his tone suggesting an intimacy she would not get sucked into.

And she would *not* think about the sexy cadence of his underlying Finnish accent.

"No need," she argued, wondering how she could have misjudged him so thoroughly. "I didn't realize that kissing me would create such difficulties for you with someone else."

His silence felt damning. A confirmation of her worst fears. She hadn't appreciated until then how much she'd hoped he would deny any such thing.

"I mean…" She trailed off, feeling foolish. Although, damn it, she wasn't the one who should feel bad. "I'm not the kind of woman who would try to steal someone else's man—"

"Whoa. Wait up a minute." He held the door open for her but stepped into her path at the last minute. She had no choice but to brush past him, his insanely muscular torso taking up twice the room of a normal man.

"Did you honestly think I would condone something like that?"

"I honestly thought you wouldn't jump to conclusions." His dark glare surprised her since she was the injured party here.

Or was she?

She was quick to form opinions. It made her an empathetic filmmaker. It also could make her a bit impulsive.

She'd barely stepped outside when someone took her bag from her shoulder, a team of equipment handlers loading the luggage into the bottom of a coach bus with dark tinted windows. A few players congregated nearby, playing Hacky Sack or listening to iPods while they waited to board. They were all well dressed, a sleek-looking group in their jackets and ties.

"What do you mean?" she asked, wondering if she could have built this up in her mind based on too little evidence. But he was the one who'd stressed that the kiss was going to create issues for him.

"Maybe we should talk about this later," Axel urged, lowering his head and his voice. "In private."

"The way we were supposed to this afternoon?" She knew she should rein herself in. But it wasn't easy to pull back now when she kept thinking about this man kissing her while he belonged to someone else.

A few heads turned in their direction.

Axel frowned. "I wasn't able to get away," he reminded her. "And are you sure you want to provide more fodder for those infernal cameras?"

She peered around, but didn't see any handhelds trained on them this time. Besides, they needed to clear the air right now, before she set foot on a bus or a plane with him.

"I most certainly don't." She didn't want to be caught on tape again any more than he did. "But when you're emphatic about how much trouble one kiss is going to make for you, I can't help but think you're involved with someone else."

6

WHOEVER SAID THAT REDHEADS had a temper wasn't kidding.

Axel couldn't believe the righteous indignation in Jennifer's eyes, knowing she had zero grounds for the accusation she'd just hurled his way. A smarter guy would probably walk away and leave her to figure out she'd been shooting in the dark with that one. But, perversely, he saw beyond the wrongheaded allegation to the surprising level of emotion behind it.

Sure Jennifer might have a temper. But she also had a passionate nature that called to him like no other woman ever had.

He was silent for so long, his nosy teammates jumped into the mix.

"Axel, you have a girlfriend?" Leandre Archambault piped up in his heavy French-Canadian accent. The power forward was sour on both Axel and Kyle Murphy since their arrival had taken him off the first line to go out onto the ice. "What woman takes a second look at the defensive goon?"

"Hey, I didn't know you were back on the market," another player called from the Hacky Sack game. "My sister wants to meet you, Ax."

They went around like that for a minute, half the guys arguing that Ax had a face only a mother could love and the other half suggesting female friends and relatives for dating options.

Through it all, Jennifer appeared confused and—the longer it went on—irritated.

"Are you saying he *doesn't* have a girlfriend?" she asked the player closest to her who just happened to be mouthy Leandre with the chip on his shoulder.

Axel crossed his arms and leaned against the side of the bus, not wanting to let on that he cared about the answer one way or another. Well, at least he didn't want to reveal any hint of weakness to Archambault.

"Are you asking as a director or because you're interested?" Leandre retorted, clearly not knowing who he was dealing with.

"Why?" Jennifer asked sweetly. "Are you pimping him out?"

The question earned a chorus of "ooohh" from the growing crowd of onlookers and Axel decided he'd had enough help from his teammates on the issue.

"Would you like to find a seat on the bus?" he asked, straightening.

"Actually, I thought I'd bring my own car to the airstrip and let some of my staff take the bus instead." She didn't seem deflated, exactly, but some of the temper had leaked away.

She must have realized she'd been wrong.

"Great. I'll ride with you." He pulled out his phone and sent a text to the coach and to his brother, Kyle, so they'd know where he was. "Where are you parked?"

"Over here." She must have arrived at the building early that morning to have nabbed such a primo spot. A new-model hybrid rental sat right next to the rear entrance. Pulling out her keys, she paused beside the vehicle. "I don't drive that much, living in Manhattan. Would you do the honors?"

She dangled her keys in front of him and he sensed a peace offering. But how could he let her off the hook so easily after she'd jumped to such a crappy conclusion about him?

"Depends." He didn't take the keys. Instead, he tugged her behind the SUV hybrid so no one in the parking lot could see them. "What will you do for me in return?"

Her green eyes went wide and he saw a spark of awareness in them. In spite of everything—getting filmed during their kiss, being dragged into this damn thing and then being wrongfully accused of two-timing her—Axel still wanted her. Really, really wanted her.

"How about if I forgive you for the nonexistent girlfriend?" Her sheepish reply didn't strike him as nearly contrite enough.

He double-checked their surroundings for cameras

and found they were thoroughly alone. His hands circled her wrists and he tugged her closer.

"You can do better than that."

"I can't imagine what you'd want." She smiled up at him, a soft yellow sundress hugging her slight curves and showing off a hint of shoulder that made him want to kiss her there.

"Then we'd better work on your imagination." Lifting a finger to trace the wide strap at her neck, he smoothed the cotton fabric over her collarbone and down the front of her chest to where it met the top of her dress.

She felt silky-smooth and warm.

She didn't bother to hide the shiver that went through her. The throb of pulse at her throat picked up speed.

"That's helping," she confessed. "I'm starting to get more ideas for making it up to you."

"Good." He slid the keys from her fingers and hit the remote fob to unlock the passenger side. "You can tell me about them—in detail—once we're safely behind locked doors and tinted windows."

"Very wise. I like this cautious side of you." She stepped into the vehicle and took her seat while he tucked the trailing hem of her skirt safely out of the way of the door.

"One of us needs to be sensible. And apparently that's the role I'm going to get stuck with in this relationship since you're way too reckless."

Her jaw dropped as if she'd never heard such an accusation.

"Impulsive, maybe. Reckless? Never."

"I wasn't the one seeing girlfriends where there are none. And I wasn't the one climbing the rafters yesterday."

"Yes, well. Much has been made out of that and it was hardly a climb at all."

He let her have the point so he could close the door and walk around to the driver's side. He started the engine and checked the rearview mirror to see if the team bus was almost ready to leave. Plenty of guys were still milling around outside.

"So I'm going to collect on that apology of yours," he promised her, wishing he had enough time and space to have her make good on it right here, right now. "And I'll explain about the phone calls I needed to make this afternoon. But first, I'd like to figure out what we're going to do to keep this thing between us out of the camera's eye. And I'd like to know why your boss wields your talent like a puppeteer. Shouldn't you be calling the shots for your project?"

"I'm not anyone's puppet." Her eyes flashed. "I'm just taking more instruction on this piece because I've been accused of not giving my films enough commercial appeal."

Axel considered her words as he watched the equipment truck pull out of the parking lot. Transporting the skates and sticks, jerseys and pads took a lot of cargo space. But they also traveled with promotional paraphernalia and signs for the walls, enough reminders of home to make the visiting team's locker room into more comfortable terrain.

"Is there any truth to that accusation?" He would far prefer that her film reach an audience of twelve.

"My subjects are usually geared to more of a niche market." She popped open the purse at her feet and pulled out a handful of trifold flyers. "My first independent film revealed the gaps in government programs for women and children. Since then I've documented the watering down of public education, the violent behaviors of youth culture—"

"And they wanted you to do a hockey documentary?" He thumbed through the brochures she handed him, each one a promotional piece on a film she'd made. "Why pick a social crusader to chronicle our sport? Unless they want you to create some kind of controversy..."

He could already imagine the media angles. Hockey had been raked over the coals for being too violent often enough. He bristled, hating the thought of negative press around the sport he lived and breathed. Settling the flyers on the console between the seats, he wondered if he'd be seeing one soon that depicted hockey as some bloodthirsty caveman sport.

"No. I might have been more excited about this piece if that had been the case." She turned around in the passenger seat to peer out the back window, her cinnamon-colored hair slipping off her shoulder as she moved. "It looks like the team bus is ready to go."

He pried his eyes from the creamy patch of skin visible at the base of her neck, then shifted the SUV into Reverse to follow his teammates to a nearby airstrip.

"So what gives?" He felt only a trace of guilt at quizzing her about the movie, knowing she probably wouldn't have talked to him so freely if they hadn't been growing closer.

But he had damn good reasons for wanting to know more and he needed to plow ahead.

"I think the producers want the sleek look and editing that I can bring to the final product since I've been receiving critical notice this year. But they're maintaining full control of the content to dictate the way I pull it together."

He mulled that over as they turned onto the highway for the short trip. "And you agreed because they enticed you with some interesting future project you couldn't refuse."

"A film about the way social media depersonalizes human interaction and becomes a sophisticated medium for cyberbullying." There was a fierceness in her voice that revealed how much the issue meant to her.

"So you're in their pocket." His sticking close to the director had backfired in a spectacular way.

For one thing, Jennifer didn't have the final say on how this documentary turned out. For another, his attraction to her had only put him more directly in front of the camera lens he'd hoped to avoid.

"I like to think of it as contractually obligated. Besides, maybe it will be easier to take a commercial approach on a topic where I'm not as personally invested."

"Yet." He slowed down for a motorcycle in front of him and then moved into the passing lane. "We'll make a hockey fan out of you at tonight's game. I think you're going to become personally invested in a hurry."

As he went to pass the bike, the rider sped up. Not in a mood to play games, Axel eased back into the driving lane. Only then did he notice the leather vest the biker wore. The all-too-familiar insignia of a notorious motorcycle club that had branches on both sides of the Atlantic—Destroyers MC.

Shit.

Axel accelerated again, telling himself it was just a coincidence. Had to be. Jen's film hadn't even been released yet and he hadn't done a damn thing to attract the attention of his former gang. Besides, he wasn't even driving his own car.

Still, his old club had intelligence connections to rival the State Department. They could have gotten wind of the documentary series long before he had. Reaching to the passenger side, he felt for Jen's buckle, making sure she was safely strapped in.

Vaguely, he realized she was still speaking—something about hockey. Too bad his brain had tuned out everything but the rider in front of him. He'd always known they'd let him walk away too easily. That they'd come to collect somehow, someday.

"Axel?" Jen's voice finally penetrated the cold fog of anxiety that surrounded him. "Are you okay? The bus is way ahead of us."

"Is it?" He remembered that isolating a driver was a precursor to running him off the road.

Was this rider trying to separate them from the team? From the rest of traffic? Back in Finland, Axel had seen the kind of violence that gang was famous for.

"There's the turn for the airport." Jennifer pointed out the windshield to the left.

Just as the long-haired giant in Destroyers leathers put on his signal to make the same turn.

"Damn it." He stifled other curses—both in English and Finnish—as the rider stayed ahead of them. Then he hit the automatic locks on the doors.

The private airstrip was on a quiet county road and the team bus was well out of sight.

"What's wrong?" Beside him, Jennifer sounded puzzled.

"The guy in front of us." Ax wiped a hand along his forehead, realizing he'd broken out in a cold sweat like a rookie goalie in his first shoot-out. "I think he wants to make trouble."

"The burly dude on the motorcycle?" She sat forward in her seat. "Someone you know?"

Without warning, the biker threw on his brakes in the middle of the driving lane.

"What is he doing?" Jennifer shouted, gripping the dashboard.

Axel swerved to avoid him. Thank God there was no oncoming traffic.

As he stepped on the gas, he glared out the passenger window at the big, muscle-bound rider who'd nearly killed them all.

The guy's expressionless face told Axel this was no accident. The man pointed his finger at them and flexed his thumb, pantomiming a gun.

"WHAT THE HELL WAS THAT all about?" Heart still racing at top speed, Jennifer clutched her chest as if she could slow her pulse with her hand. "Who was that and why does he have a death wish?"

She turned in her seat to watch the brain-addled biker dude out the back window. He just sat there in the middle of the road, straddling his bike and staring after them. Why didn't he move out of the lane before another car came along?

"It's a long story." Axel's cool, distant voice brought her head around.

"So? We've got nothing to do but talk on the way up to Montreal."

"I am not sharing this with the team." He gripped the wheel hard, the obvious tension in his posture making her remember something from the incident. His accent softened when he spoke slowly. Deliberately. He'd been in the U.S. for the last year of high school and all of college, but the foreign cadence still came through.

"Why did he fake shoot you with the finger gesture like an eight-year-old? Was that some kind of sick joke?" Her thoughts went to her sister, who had weathered all kinds of bullying and threats at her school. Jennifer knew plenty about the subtle coercions girls used on one another to maintain their power and social standing. But she was out of her element with the more overt intimidation tactics men used.

"*Reader's Digest* version—I was in a motorcycle club in Finland when I was a teenage moron. It's more like a gang than a club—once you're in you do not get out."

Up ahead, the airstrip became visible. The sight of civilization made her breathe easier and her heart rate slowed.

"He was threatening you." She didn't understand all the details but she knew that much. And this time she wasn't jumping to conclusions.

"I am not sure what he wanted. I've never seen him before." Axel's jaw flexed when he spoke, his whole body tense as he steered them through the main gate. "But he was definitely sending me a message that I've pissed off the powers that be in the organization. I'm guessing it has something to do with this film you're making."

"How would they know about the film? Furthermore, why would it upset them so much they felt the need to risk that biker's life to send their message?" Whatever happened to phone calls? And what if Axel really was in danger?

Jennifer's stomach knotted at the thought. She'd only just met him, but already she felt a powerful connection to him. Sure, she might not want to act on it. *Shouldn't* act on it. But the pull of it was undeniable.

The team bus unloaded near the plane while Axel parked the SUV.

"I don't think the Destroyers are going to appreciate seeing my lifestyle broadcast to twenty different countries while they're still scrapping over drug territories in Helsinki. I had a sense from the moment I walked away that they'd come back for me once I achieved some fame and social standing."

"To steal from you? Blackmail you? And how involved were you with this group, by the way?" She was trying to get as many details from him as possible before they boarded the plane.

She could see why he wouldn't want to discuss it in a public forum. Besides, she needed to meet with her crew and edit some raw film footage on the trip to Montreal.

"I ran messages and—before I was old enough to know what I was doing—I'm sure I must have run drugs, too." He handed her back her keys. "I have no idea what they want from me now, but I'm obviously back on their radar."

She slid the keys in her purse, stunned.

"You were part of a gang." She envisioned hockey players as pampered athletes, funded by families with the money to drive their kids to far-flung games to hone their skills. She knew from an internet search the night before that his foster family in the U.S. was wealthy and influential, owning a global hotel conglomerate. "How old were you?"

"Eight when I first started going to the clubhouse with my stepfather. By the time he left my mother three years later, I knew better than to take a package with me when I ran messages and I'd quit doing that part of it, but I was already well entrenched." He levered open the driver's-side door. "We'd better get going. We don't want to miss the plane."

Jennifer remained in her seat, still processing this new piece of information that didn't fit with her image of Axel Rankin at all.

A shiver of unease went through her. "This documentary could be really dangerous for you." Now she understood his vocal opposition to her project. His resentment about showing her around the practice arena that day.

"I was on the phone all afternoon talking to my foster family to make sure they know I could be back on the gang's radar after the documentary airs. But as it turns out, I'm already back in the crosshairs."

Cold dread knotted in her stomach.

"You really think they might—" She swallowed hard, her throat dry. "Try to hurt you?"

"At this point, that's the least of my concerns." He covered her hand with his, his blue eyes darker than usual. "I'm more worried that this film may be dangerous for *you*. When we come back to Philadelphia two days from now, you need to be careful."

7

Philadelphia 2, Montreal 1.

Vincent Girard liked the look of the numbers on the scoreboard as he skated off the ice the next afternoon following a narrow win in overtime. The team's play-maker, Kyle Murphy, had made the game-winning goal with eighteen seconds to spare, the shot fed to him on a sweet pass by his foster brother, Axel. The two of them were something to see in a game situation—their passes to each other did not miss.

The arena was quiet after the hometown team's loss. Most fans shuffled toward the exits, but a few Philly fans stuck around to cheer for the Phantoms as they filed off the ice toward the tunnel that would take them into the visitors' locker room. Vinny's eyes went to the stands in search of Chelsea, the way they did after every game.

What kind of guy waited nine months to make a move? He kept thinking she'd come around—open her eyes to his obvious attraction—sooner or later. But the waiting was killing him and it was becoming clear that she'd never see he wanted more unless he pushed.

A big freaking gamble when she'd made it known the players were like brothers to her, nothing more. He risked a lot here. Risked losing her completely.

"Way to go, Vinny!" a woman shouted, and he recognized Misty's singsong voice above him as he neared the tunnel.

Peering up through the flutter of waving programs where fans tried to entice players to give autographs, he saw Chelsea and her friends. Misty was in front, pushing through the small crowd to claim a spot at the rail. Chelsea, Rosa and Keiko circled behind her. And was it his imagination, or did Chelsea hang back more than usual tonight?

He'd started to implement his more assertive strategy with her today when he'd given her the GPS. Had she started retreating from him already?

"Thanks, Misty." He lifted a hand to return her high five, pausing near the rail while the other guys milled around signing autographs and hats. "How did you make out on the trip up here? Did you get good directions?"

He knew the unit he'd bought was state-of-the-art, but until you got familiar with the settings, GPS devices could lead you down some unusual paths. His GPS in Minnesota had expected him to travel through a precarious mountain pass in January to deliver hay to a customer. The maps didn't always take seasonal roads or construction into account.

"I'll let Chelsea tell you about it." Misty tugged her friend toward the rail while she stepped back, obviously wise to his attraction. "No hurry, Chels. We're going to help the promo guys pack up the Phantoms hats."

Sweat dripped in Vinny's left eye, but the toll of the game didn't detract from his body's automatic response to the woman he'd wanted for months.

Chelsea Durant wasn't particularly tall—five foot six, maybe—but she carried herself with strength and elegance. Her posture was perfect, her shoulders squared. Despite being a shy woman—at least with men—she never walked with her head down. Her chin tilted up, fierce determination and pride broadcast for all to see.

His very first night on the ice as an NHL player had landed him in an unwise fight with another player, giving the opposing team a key power play that led to a goal against the Phantoms. He'd also missed two passes, one of which led to a turnover.

It hadn't been pretty. After the game, some wise-guy fan had told him to go back to Minnesota. Then, out of nowhere, Chelsea had butted her way in front of the guy. She suggested *he* go to Minnesota instead, and leave the job of cheering on the Phantoms to real fans.

"You had a great game," Chelsea told him now, leaning down over the rail in a way that made his heart beat faster.

She reached for him, surprising the hell out of him. Had she gotten the message? Returned his interest?

Then, while he held his breath, she brushed the sweat from his eye and her hand came away bloody.

"You need to get that cut stitched," she told him, her light brown eyebrows knitted in concern. "I was surprised they didn't take you out of the game. What was Nico thinking?"

While she grumbled about the coach's need to win at all costs, Vinny realized it had been blood dripping in his eye more than sweat.

"It's nothing." He didn't want to get noticed for opening a vein.

A few of his teammates brushed past him, returning to the locker room. The coach would want to talk to them all before they showered and changed into street clothes.

"It's not nothing. That's three stitches at least." She reached for him again and this time, he closed his eyes, willing her hands to linger. "You need to see the medic."

When her touch came, it was soft. Gentle. She swiped at a damp spot above his eye, her fingers smoothing along his temple toward his helmet.

"I'll get it stitched if you'll have dinner with me."

Her hand stilled on his face. He opened his eyes.

She looked so surprised and wary that he debated rephrasing the invitation, including other people in a group meal. But he'd done that six months ago and it hadn't gotten him anywhere. He needed time alone with her.

"I... That is, the girls and I were going to drive to New York tonight."

She snatched back her fingers suddenly, as if she'd only just realized she still touched him. He was pretty sure he could have waxed poetic for a few hours about how much he wanted her hands on him again, but he didn't think some big romantic outpouring was going to advance his cause.

"So wait an hour or two. You need to eat."

"I don't want to get sleepy on the road tonight if I get a late start." She hadn't said "no" outright yet. Was it so pathetic that he took this as a good sign?

"You can call me from the road later if you feel tired and we'll talk. I'll keep you awake."

God knows, he'd lost plenty of sleep to thinking about her before. He'd gladly trade the rest for a chance to hear her voice in his ear in the middle of the night.

Around them, the last of the players went inside and some of the other fans turned his way, no doubt thinking he was there to sign autographs, too.

Normally, he was happy to stick around and sign. But right now he kept his eyes on Chelsea, willing her to say yes.

"I don't know, Vincent." She bit her lip, her dark eyes filled with worry. "I'm not like the other girls around here." She took a deep breath. "I don't really date or anything, so…"

"I just want to talk." He didn't care that he was hanging his personal life out for all the world to see. For twenty fans to dissect and—of course—an ever-present camera guy to record. But he did lower his voice when he remembered the videographer must still be behind him. "Get to know you. Clothes stay on, cross my heart, Boy Scout promise and I really was one, Eagle Scout no less. Wanna see my badges?"

He'd worry about dating another day.

She sucked in a gasp and he knew a moment's dread that she was going to slam the door in his face forever.

Instead, she reached out once more to stop the blood flow from his eyebrow down into his eye.

"I'll go." The wariness on her face had been replaced with that fierce determination that he recognized as a core part of her character, a compelling piece of her personality that attracted him so thoroughly. "But you're going to see the medic right now."

He meant to thank her and leave. Count his blessings and not be greedy for more.

But he ended up covering her hand with his, pressing her touch to his face for a moment before he shifted her fingers down to his mouth. Pushing his luck when he should just be grateful for her consent, he brushed a kiss into the soft center of her palm.

Savoring the taste of her on his lips, he took off into the tunnel and hoped she would really show up for dinner. Because after waiting nine months for Chelsea Durant, Vinny didn't think he could delay being with her another minute.

Can I come to your room?

Jennifer erased the text rather than sending it. It was half an hour after Axel's game, and she was alone in her hotel room. She'd just finished typing her notes about the win over Montreal, already full of ideas for narration of the exciting overtime defeat. But she wasn't as skilled with words when it came to texting Axel. Her attempts to see him tonight sounded so sordid. But honestly, she just needed a private place to speak to Axel where the camera guys wouldn't spot them.

Still, she understood the risks of being alone with the sexy Finn. He'd told her that he didn't plan to stop kissing her. Just that he'd make sure they were behind locked doors.

The memory of that conversation still made her pulse race. She shivered at the thought of where this unwise relationship was headed. Because in spite of the attraction, she did *not* want to be some decorative accessory on the arm of a successful athlete. Big-time sports stars were notorious for womanizing and living large. She didn't want any part of the jet-set lifestyle with houses on both coasts and a garage full of cars that were never driven more than two miles.

Jennifer considered herself a social activist, not a footnote in the society pages.

Is there anywhere we can speak privately? she typed, thinking that sounded more dignified. Less provocative.

Hitting Send on her phone, she turned her attention back to her laptop and the raw footage of the game her crew had uploaded to a shared site. Part of her wanted to zoom in on Ax when he raced up the ice at lightning speed, giving him the credit that his talents warranted.

But how could she highlight a man who might be hunted by a biker gang with a vendetta? Using the footage could endanger him.

Beside her, the cell phone vibrated and she lifted it to see an incoming message.

On my way to your room now.

Anticipation slid through her veins, slow and smoky. He'd carried her bag to her room for her the night before, after the plane had landed in Montreal. So he must remember the number. She hadn't been able to sit with him on the flight, needing that time with her film crew to work on editing rough footage of their first documentary episode, which would air in three days. The network dictated the fast turnaround time, requiring the story lines to be current and to reflect the most recent games.

That meant there were two more days until that kiss aired for all the world to see. Two days before her credibility as a director took a hit and her status as a social activist fell into question. After all, she'd locked lips with an affluent athlete whose position with the powerful international Murphy Resorts Corporation was assured after his sports career. Axel Rankin was part of the elite that she loved to battle against.

The knock at her door startled her.

Breath rushed from her lungs. She knew that as she opened that door, opposing worldviews and backgrounds wouldn't matter. Logic didn't come into play with how she felt about Axel, no matter how much she wanted to sweep her feelings under the rug.

"Hurry," came a low voice from the hallway. "I think one of your camera guys is coming up the stairs."

Crap.

She unbolted the lock and pulled the door wide, keeping an eye out for the blinking red record light. Luckily, the corridor remained quiet as Ax brushed past her into the narrow foyer leading into her room.

"Hi," she said lamely, locking the door and turning to face him. "Great game."

Back against the wall, she stared at him in the dim room, only the TV and her laptop on the bed providing any light. He wore khakis and a casual blue button-down, the sleeves rolled up to reveal strong forearms. She remembered the feel of those arms around her when he'd caught her climbing down from the rafters two days ago. The memory made her skin tighten and hum with awareness. He smelled clean and yummy, his hair still damp from a shower.

She curled her hands into fists at her sides to keep from tugging him closer.

"I'm having the best season of my career," he admitted, though he seemed a little annoyed about it.

Was she reading him wrong?

"That's terrific." She was the queen of scintillating conversation tonight, wasn't she? But it took all her brainpower to keep her hands off him.

"It should be." His jaw flexed as he stared at her, some inner turmoil seething beneath the surface.

"But?"

"But I'm going to mess it up by getting involved with a woman."

She felt light-headed suddenly. Her blood seemed to rush somewhere, but she couldn't tell where it was going in such a hurry. She only knew her knees felt like jelly and her temples kind of tingled.

"How do you know that will hurt your season?" She could hardly hear the words she spoke since her heart thudded with deafening thumps.

"Any woman would be a distraction from the game,

and you?" He stepped closer. "You're distraction to the hundredth power."

"We…" Her mouth went dry and she couldn't speak. She had to lick her lips to get the words out. "We should discuss that."

His gaze zeroed in on her lips and she became hyperaware of the moisture drying there. Damned if she didn't feel her heartbeat pound there, too, her lower lip trembling with the effect.

"Unfortunately, I don't think I can do anything besides kiss you right now." His left hand sifted through her curls, one finger twining around a piece.

She swayed toward him, powerless to hold back.

"Did you notice I locked the door?"

His hand curved around the nape of her neck, warm and commanding, but gentle all the same. Her head tipped back, eyes glued to his as he circled her waist with one arm.

"I've been thinking about having you behind a locked door at least once a minute for the past forty-eight hours." His voice hit a husky note that reverberated through her.

Fingers uncurling, she lifted her arms to slide them around his neck, her breasts meeting the hard wall of his chest.

"Maybe just this once, we could see what happens. Work it out of our systems," she suggested.

He felt so good against her that she responded on contact. Heat flooded her sex and her breasts, the nerve endings there keenly sensitive to his slightest movement.

"You're delusional," he whispered so softly, so sweetly, he could have been whispering words of eternal love. "Once is never going to be enough."

"That sounds like a promise," she murmured, dying for a taste of him.

"A personal guarantee." His mouth grazed hers as he spoke, his minty breath warm on her lips.

Restraint vanished. Jennifer arched up on her toes and pressed her lips to his, needing a taste of him. His hand spanned her lower back, fingers splayed against her cotton shorts and the old T-shirt she'd put on after the game. The soft fabric didn't begin to stanch the heat of his touch, his hand warming her skin beneath.

Sensation flowed up her spine, his touch sealing her to him. All those places her body touched him seemed to melt on contact, everything inside her turning warm and liquid.

A hungry purr tickled her throat and she couldn't stifle the needy sound. Axel filled her senses from the stroke of his tongue over hers to the silky slide of his lower lip along her mouth. At the base of her neck, his hand massaged circles beneath her hair before straying down her back just beneath the neckline of her T-shirt.

Pleasure bloomed everywhere, so intense she had to close her eyes and savor the moment and the man. The scent of him filled her nostrils, musky and male, until she couldn't wait for more of him. Releasing his neck, she eased back to smooth her fingers down well-defined pecs. His heart thumped hard beneath her palm, the vibration urging her fingers over the buttons on his shirt.

One by one she slid the fastenings free, finding a soft T-shirt beneath the button-down. Fumbling at the shirt hem, she tugged the fabric from his trousers, moving to his belt to ease the way.

"Let me," he offered, breaking the kiss to undo the buckle and send both shirts to the floor.

He leaned in again to kiss her, but she pinned his shoulders with her hands, her gaze raking over him.

"Wow." Her reverent perusal of his chest was more than testament to how long it'd been since she'd been with a man. It was the same response a woman might give any honed athlete with his shirt off, respect for a human body that was fulfilling every bit of its physical potential.

"When do I get to ogle you?" he teased, hooking one finger in the V-neck of her T-shirt. "I'm dying to return the favor."

She knew a rare moment of reticence.

"I'm not exactly centerfold material."

His eyes met hers. Serious. Simmering with heat.

"Who wants an airbrushed fake when I'm standing next to the red-hot real thing?"

A smile kicked up one side of her mouth.

"Oh." Just like that, she felt sexy all over. "In that case, be my guest."

He studied her for a moment, as if assuring himself she meant it. But he didn't undress her right away. Instead, his gaze dropped to the neckline of her shirt, now askew from where he'd tugged at it. Moving closer, he angled over her to brush a kiss at the base of her throat, his tongue darting out to stroke a slick path lower.

Pleasure sparked and fanned heat along her skin. Her breasts crested in taut peaks beneath her bra.

"I mean it," she urged, shrugging one shoulder to work the fabric of her shirt off that side. "I'm so ready."

And then his hands were there, at her waist, skimming the top up and off her until she wore just a plain cotton bra built for work rather than play.

Not that Axel seemed to notice. His eyes devoured her and his hands followed the same path, curling around her waist and palming her belly until he'd touched everywhere but her aching breasts. Awkwardly, she wriggled out of the straps, leaving the fabric cups perched precariously on her curves.

With a groan of capitulation, he gripped her hip and dragged her closer, cradling a breast in his hand.

"Beautiful," he murmured. "Gorgeous. Perfect." He put his mouth where the compliments were, his lips falling to the rounded top of one mound as he kneaded her in one hand.

Sensation swamped her and she leaned limply against the door to the hallway, counting on his arm at her waist to keep her upright. She moaned deep in her throat, her fingers skimming his close-cropped hair while he laved a trail of kisses in spiraling circles that neared one taut nipple.

Need wound tight inside her, her panties damp with anticipation when he hadn't even touched her there. If anything, he kept his hips at too much of a distance when she was this hungry for him.

Arching her back, she forced the issue, centering her breast at his mouth until he licked a tantalizing circle around and around her there. When at last he drew on her, she whimpered shamelessly, the sweet fulfillment too exquisite for words.

Head tossed back, she writhed against him, her fingers searching for the fastenings of his fly. She freed one. Two. But before she could go any further, he hitched an arm beneath her thighs and swept her off her feet.

Axel wanted to do this right.

He hadn't necessarily planned to jump on her the moment he walked through the door tonight, but he'd known this moment was inevitable and he'd been prepared. He had no intentions of taking her fast and hard against a hotel room door.

Fast and hard in a hotel bed is more civilized? his wiseass conscience nagged. But the spark he felt with Jennifer was like nothing he'd ever known.

Settling her on the white duvet of the king-size bed, he moved her laptop to the floor to give them more room. Her gorgeous breasts were the perfect handful and he couldn't take his eyes off her body. Leaning over her, he unhooked her bra and peeled the straps the rest of the way off her arms.

"Keep going," she urged, moving her hips in mouthwatering invitation. "I want everything off."

"I am so on the same page." He didn't know if she meant her clothes or his, but his hands went to her cotton shorts first, even though the buttons on his fly were going to be imprinted on his Johnson for the remainder of his days.

He needed to see the rest of her. Besides, once his pants came off, his restraint would be seriously compromised.

Her skin was soft and warm when he cupped her hip. She was pale everywhere, a few freckles dotting the creamy texture. He kissed just above the waistband of the shorts, inhaling the faint scent of lilies of the valley. He licked a path to her navel, his tongue swirling around there the way he'd like to kiss her between her thighs.

Soon.

Her hips rocked against the bed and a soft, strangled sound came from her lips. Hard to believe she wanted this as badly as he did, but her fingers bunched the fabric of the duvet in a tense grip and her breath came in sexy little gasps.

Stripping off her shorts and her underwear in one swipe, he fought the urge to bury himself in her then and there. The only thing holding him back was the cotton twill of half-buttoned khakis.

He stretched out over her, keeping the barrier in place. He wasn't going to rush this and he had so much to savor. Pleasure.

"When do I get to ogle *you?*" she whispered, tossing his words back at him.

Her fingers latched on to the waist of his trousers, her touch so close to where he needed it that his breath stuck in his lungs.

He tried to speak but the words were garbled. Who could be coherent with a naked goddess skimming the front of his pants?

She smiled, sexy and knowing, her red curls sliding behind her shoulder as she shifted to her side. They lay facing each other on the big bed.

"I mean it," she urged, her hand edging nearer to the throbbing length of him. "I'm not a patient woman."

"You should work on that," he bit out, mustering all his willpower to rein himself in.

"One day I will, but not tonight." She placed kisses along his shoulder.

Her fingers progressed with painstaking slowness on the last of the fastenings, an occasional knuckle brushing against him and making him damn near see stars. Fireworks, maybe. He was so on edge the slightest thing could set him off.

"You win." He grappled for his wallet in his back pocket, finding a condom inside and slapping it on the bed. "I don't stand a chance against all that redheaded determination."

She released his pants to clutch the condom, waving it over her head like a trophy.

"We both win!" she exclaimed, unwrapping it while he shed his pants and his boxers. When her eyes dipped south, she dropped the prophylactic. "But I really, really win."

Her wide-eyed gaze flattered the hell out of him, but by now, he couldn't play teasing games with her. Need unfurled at the base of his spine, clawing up his back.

Gently, he captured her lips, kissing her until she went pliant, lying back on the mattress. He trapped one thigh with his, holding her where he wanted her. She tasted so good, so sweet. When he smoothed a touch across her hip and down her belly, her kisses grew more urgent. She twisted beneath him, wriggling until he cupped her sex. Tested her warmth with a finger.

Any worry about her being ready for him evaporated. He rolled on the condom then entered her in one long stroke. Her fingers dug into his shoulders, a welcome pain, even as she whispered frantic demands for more. Now. Faster.

"One day," he promised, shifting slowly inside her, "we'll do everything just the way you want. But not now. Not tonight."

Not when he'd been without a woman all season. When he'd been without *her* his whole life.

She nodded in the dimness, eyes passion-dazed and her mouth swollen from his kisses.

"I'll have you any way I can."

Her words drove him crazy even when he'd succeeded in stilling her beautiful body. His release churned inside him, demanding completion. Gritting his teeth against it, he pumped his hips harder. Faster.

In the half light, she smiled. Her head thrown back, she cried out, holding on to him with the same fierceness he felt. Her hips bucked wildly, breasts bouncing until he captured one with his palm and tweaked the nipple.

Her orgasm came hard and fast. She shouted. Gasped. Squeezed him tight between her legs.

At last, he gave in to the pleasure, his own release racking his body for endless moments. Afterward, temporarily satisfied and drained, he held her until their bodies cooled and he had to wrap the duvet around them.

Speaking wasn't an option. He couldn't begin to think about how he felt or what it all meant that they'd been together. For now, he just wanted to lie beside her. Touch her. Know her.

There would be time enough tomorrow to wonder how they could avoid the cameras and keep her safe while his old gang sought retribution. Until then, he planned to savor every moment of pleasure he could with this sexy, strong-willed dynamo who'd barreled into his life when he'd least expected it.

8

CHELSEA PUSHED A LETTUCE leaf around her plate, trying to focus on what Vincent was saying instead of thinking about the fact that she'd never had dinner alone with a guy. Ever.

She wouldn't have gone with him, either, except that he was one of the players. The first player who'd spoken to her and made her feel like a valued part of the team's fan base. She'd started following the Phantoms because she loved the confined aggression of the sport. The rules and order that tempered physical conflict. It appealed to her hidden desire to kick ass and take names in a world that was too often cruel and unfair.

Now, finishing her Cobb salad in a quiet corner of the hotel's restaurant, she listened to Vincent's story from his teenage years about a cow who'd escaped an enclosure and wandered out into a deep ravine. He'd wrangled the fourteen-hundred-pound beast out the night before his high school hockey playoffs. She liked his stories of a life that seemed straight out of the pages of a kids' book, complete with farm animals and morals, challenges and lessons. Order ruled Vinny's world, just as it ruled hockey.

"So how did you do in the playoffs?" she asked, focusing on his stitched forehead now that she had no more food to distract her.

He passed his plate to the hovering waiter and she was relieved to see he'd eaten every last bite, too. She had huge issues with wasting food from back in the days when she'd begged at the back doors of restaurants at closing time.

"I scored a hat trick and we advanced to the next round." He grinned, the smile crinkling the skin around his eyes. "My whole team knew that I'd been awake all night, and I wanted to make sure no one thought I was dragging the team down by being unprepared for the game."

His good humor was infectious, making her smile, too. That in itself was pretty amazing given how nervous she'd been about spending time with him tonight. Alone.

Especially after he'd kissed the palm of her hand. Just thinking about that moment made her skin tingle. Beneath the linen tablecloth, she twined her fingers together and tried to squeeze away the sensation that still lingered there.

"You proved your point." Her gaze connected with his and held until the clinking of silverware and conversations around them faded.

Warmth stirred inside her, making her self-conscious.

"It took me a while to learn I didn't need to constantly prove myself." He drummed his fingers on the table for a moment before he added, "Although I'm willing to do it again if I need to."

"I'm sure you don't need to prove anything to the team. You've already—"

"To you." He snagged the attention of a passing waitress to ask for more water, giving Chelsea more physical space even as he crowded her thoughts with a notion that was both frightening and compelling at the same time. "I'm willing to prove myself to you, Chels. I just want a chance to know you better."

The center of her palm throbbed where he'd kissed her, that sensitive patch of flesh reminding her that she couldn't suppress her needs as a woman forever. Then again, how could she expect a great guy like Vinny to wait around while she battled old demons that didn't have anything to do with him?

"I had fun tonight," she started, not wanting to damage their friendship. "And you're a great guy. I know that. So it wouldn't be fair to ask you to—"

"Ask me anything." He leaned forward again, elbows on the table, his hazel eyes more brown than green tonight in the flickering candlelight from a single white taper surrounded by fresh daisies.

His tone seemed so earnest that, for a moment, she forgot her point. What would it be like to be with someone so open? So willing to take a chance?

"I can't. I wouldn't feel right seeing you like this and knowing you had expectations of me that I'm not comfortable...fulfilling." Although, considering how enticing that one kiss to her hand had been, she had the feeling she would dream about that and more with him tonight.

Just because she had sexual hang-ups didn't mean she'd lost her carnal appetites.

"First of all, I have no expectations. I have hopes. Those are very different things." He kept his voice low as the waitress passed them with an empty tray on her way to the kitchen.

"I would be a huge disappointment for you." She'd kept the guys on the team at arm's length for good reason. She wouldn't want to sacrifice her special relationship with the Phantoms as a whole just because she got romantically entangled with one of them.

It went without saying that romantic entanglements would end in disaster, right? Although she had to admit, Vinny seemed like the patient sort.

"The only thing that's going to disappoint me is if I let you slip away without telling you how much I like you."

Her heart picked up speed, but in a good way. This was different from the times her heart raced during the fight-or-flight response, which was what she usually felt when a man got too close or pushed for more from her.

"You don't even know me," she reminded him, reaching for her wallet as the waitress came back with their check.

"I invited you," he insisted, gently steering her hand

back into her purse before she could open her wallet. "I'm buying."

The busy young waitress seemed to conspire with him, snatching his credit card from his hand and flouncing off with the check.

"Thank you." Chelsea tried to let it go, thinking Vinny shouldn't have to cope with more than one of her hang-ups at a time. And right now, she was most concerned with settling the matter of future dates.

Or whatever they were calling them.

"And I do know you. Better than you realize."

"Really?" She couldn't keep the skepticism out of her voice.

"I know you drink three coffees a day and you like to buy them at a diner near the rink because the money goes to the old guy who runs the place instead of a faceless corporation."

"I've probably recommended Arnie's Coffee to the players a few times." Although, to Vinny's credit, that had been ages ago.

He appeared undaunted. In fact, he had her caffeine addiction already ticked off on the finger of his broad right hand.

"You worked at the same department store as Misty until you took the job in the Phantoms gift shop." He leaned back into his seat, his wide shoulders making a depression in the red leather bolster. "You like the hours, but you've almost got your BSc in counseling from taking online courses in your free time. And you hope to use that degree in your quest to open a women's shelter."

Stunned, she didn't even know what to say as the waitress returned with mints and a receipt.

"Did Misty tell you that?" she asked once they were alone again. Chelsea hadn't revealed that dream with anyone but the other women who followed the team with her. Other women who'd shared the hellish nightmare of homelessness at a young age.

"No." He relaxed his hands that had been keeping track of his knowledge of her. "I was in that business development class with you online last fall. Didn't you ever look at the roster?"

She remembered a student in the discussion forums that posted as "Vincent" but not in a million years would she have guessed it was this Vincent. The one who had a full-time, lucrative career in the best hockey league in the world.

"Why on earth would you take business development online?" He could afford an Ivy League education. "I thought you graduated from Michigan State?"

"I decided I want an MBA even though I majored in math. I'm taking some extra business classes to get into an MBA program."

She processed that, more curious by the minute about this man who was full of surprises.

"I wrote a business plan for a women's shelter in that class, didn't I?" She'd been proud of it, and what had started out as a simple project really took on a life of its own. "The assignment to develop the plan made me see

how many ideas I could bring to something like that."
Biting her lip, she hesitated for a moment before she
blurted, "You must have heard I was homeless for a long
time as a teenager."

It was such a huge part of her that anyone she spent
time with was bound to find out sooner or later. She'd
rather know up front if he couldn't handle that. And as
much as she told herself that those who minded didn't
matter, she found herself holding her breath, hoping
Vinny wouldn't think less of her.

"I know," he said quietly. "And it floors me to think
how hard it must have been to go from that kind of
struggle to where you are now."

He looked at her with genuine admiration in his eyes.
It was so sincere that she felt a distinct tug in her heart.
Pride, maybe. Or tenderness for someone who could see
beyond the Homeless label.

The piano player who started his first set in the front
of the restaurant didn't begin to distract her from the pull
she felt toward Vincent Girard. Turning him down would
have been like pushing water uphill, and she didn't think
she could muster the will.

Especially as she became aware of his knee brushing
hers under the table. An electric spark jumped from that
point of contact to warm her skin all over.

"Thank you." Suddenly shy about whatever was happening between them, she folded her napkin over her
clean knife, wrapping the silverware in the linen. "It
wasn't easy. And it left scars." Her eyes went to his,
gauging his reaction, but as always, he looked at her with

respect. Warmth. Friendship. She took a deep breath before she continued. "But I'm really proud that I found a new life for myself."

His hand covered hers, his thumb reaching around to the underside of her palm and stroking her there, right where he'd kissed her earlier. The effect was dizzying, making her light-headed. Partly because she liked the way it felt. But she was also a little giddy from the fact that it seemed normal. Safe and exciting at the same time.

How did he do that?

"I hope one day you'll trust me enough to tell me how you did it." He circled that place on her palm, as if he was enjoying the memory of the kiss as much as she was. "But for now, I'm just hoping you'll have dinner with me again soon. Not tomorrow because of the game. But maybe when we get back to Philly the next day."

She had twenty other Phantom players on speed dial in case she freaked out and needed a bodyguard. But she already knew she wouldn't. Not with Vincent. The insistent thump of her heartbeat in her chest and the tingle in her skin told her that she would be looking forward to seeing Vinny alone again.

So much so that she did something completely amazing and squeezed his hand back.

"I'd really like that."

JENNIFER SERIOUSLY HOPED the morning never arrived.

She lay tucked against Axel on top of the plush hotel bed, the white duvet soft against the outside of her thigh while Axel's leg was warm and raspy against the inside. Her cheek fit perfectly just beneath his heart and she heard it thump steadily in one ear. The TV still glowed blue with a campy horror flick in the background, all the scariest bits removed for a more sensitive audience, apparently.

"I love watching movies with the sound off," she said, always happy to talk about film. Besides, she wasn't ready to talk about anything substantial with Ax yet.

The time would come soon enough when they'd have to face the ticking clock on a relationship with an end already in sight when she went back to New York.

"Why?" He brushed her hair off her temple, his big, broad palm so gentle it gave her goose bumps.

"As a filmmaker, I see the images better that way. I can think more about the visuals and the camera angles when I'm not distracted by the story." She pointed to the screen where the antagonist—a mutant zombie killing everyone in the local high school—stood on top of a bridge and glared down at his next meal. "Like right there? They shot that from below the zombie to emphasize his power and her helplessness. And you see how big his shadow is behind him?"

"Believe me, I've known some people who cast a big shadow, people who have a powerful presence. I get what that means." He brushed a kiss on the top of her hair where he lay with his head propped on a pillow. "But I wouldn't have thought about it if you hadn't pointed it out. You must really enjoy your job."

"I feel fortunate to do work I love every day. It's even

better when, at the same time, I can make the art meaningful." She traced a thick rope of scar tissue on his arm and wondered where he'd gotten it.

"I'm anxious to find out how you're going to make the hockey documentary meaningful. But tell me more about the social media film you want to make. Why are you so gung ho about that one?"

She counted three steady beats of his heart before she answered.

"My younger sister was the victim of cyberbullying." She still couldn't think about those girls who'd tricked Julia without getting angry all over again. "Julia is fifteen and last fall she had a crush on an older boy. Somehow, a toxic clique of junior girls found out about it and they created a Facebook page for him. They took turns sending her messages, posing as the boy and pretending to like her."

He kept up the even stroke along her temple, never even flinching when the zombie jumped out of the woods on the television screen. She liked that steadiness.

"Poor kid. As if growing up wasn't tough enough."

"She didn't find out until weeks later when the girls printed out all Julia's private messages to the kid and circulated them around the school. The guy was as embarrassed as she was, and he didn't react well, which made the humiliation even tougher to bear for Julia." He'd distanced himself from the whole thing, denouncing Julia as a band nerd, much to the delight of her tormentors.

Jennifer had tried to assure Julia that she would be playing violin at Carnegie Hall long after the girls in the evil clique had descended into desperate suburban lives, having affairs with their best friends' husbands. But the scenario she painted had done little to cheer her sister.

"How is she doing now?" Axel shifted the blankets, making sure Jen was covered.

"I helped her switch schools." She leaned back so she could see his face, resettling on the pillow beside him. "I had hoped she would stay and fight through it, but she just wanted to get away. She's at a new school now and she seems to have put it behind her."

Jennifer, on the other hand, resented the prank phone calls and ridiculing "love letters" that continued to show up in her sister's mailbox back home.

Axel frowned. "How is she going to feel when you make your film? She won't view that as dredging up a painful event in the past?"

"No." Although the thought had certainly crossed Jen's mind. "I have to think she'll be glad to save some other girls from the heartache she's experienced, even if the film isn't released until next fall."

"Have you asked her?" he pressed.

"No. But she doesn't like to talk about that whole episode in her life. This might have more impact if I can show her some of the final edits." When it was honed and shaped into a powerful piece of art.

"You know your sister better than I do, obviously." He slid the remote control back onto the nightstand even though the film wasn't done yet. "But when *I* made enemies at school, I didn't appreciate anyone trying to fight my battles. Sometimes the older kids in the motorcycle club would want to step in, and that always ticked me off."

She hoped that wouldn't be the case with Julia and wondered if it warranted a conversation with her sister before Jen jumped in with both feet. For now, however, she was already thinking about another facet of what Axel had said.

"There were other school-age kids in that group? In your gang?" She'd wondered about that biker who'd nearly run them off the road earlier. "I just assumed you were the anomaly."

"Recruiters had a field day in the poor high schools. Kids either got into drugs or motorcycles, often both. But mostly they just craved the security of friends. The family they never had."

"Yet, from what I've read about you online, you found a supportive family when you came to the States." How had he navigated the wealthy, privileged world of the prominent Murphy clan when he'd come from such a gritty background?

"I owe my career to the Murphys." He spoke with a reverence she hadn't heard from him before. "I wouldn't have been playing recreational hockey the year I met Kyle except that some kid on the team got hurt and a camp director sought me out because I was big and could skate. At that level, they didn't ask for much more from a defenseman."

"So you hadn't even played hockey before then?" Her hands roamed his biceps, marveling at the years of muscle that had built there since those days. "I thought hockey was the kind of sport you were born into. Don't a lot of kids play it by the time they're in elementary school?"

"Yes, but you don't have to. And I skated on the ponds in Finland where I grew up. Lots of kids do. Hockey is a backyard sport there."

"Okay, so you got tapped by a youth coach to fill in. Then what?" The filmmaker in her needed to visualize the story.

"I played a good game defensively. But a kid on their team got pissed when I checked him into the boards. He came back with a fist that knocked out one of my teeth. That was my introduction to Kyle Murphy."

"You're kidding." She'd seen Kyle play tonight. Had read about him in the days leading up to the game. He was all about precision and timing. Speed and agility. "He doesn't strike me as the brute type."

"Unlike me, right?" He flexed a muscle to emphasize the point and she couldn't help but remember what it felt like to be wrapped up in all that strength.

"I just pictured you being the victor in that fight." She molded her fingers to the bulge of his upper arm, amazed how unyielding it felt.

"All of my foster brothers are fierce competitors. They don't look at how big the obstacle is. They just knock it down. And you know, it made me realize that some of my own teammates might have held back around me because of the—"

"Gang connection." She didn't doubt it for a minute.

"No one wants to cross the guy whose friends carry guns."

"Right. But Kyle didn't know. And possibly even if he had, he wouldn't have cared. He plays to win." Axel released the muscle he'd been making and slipped a hand beneath the covers to skim over her bare hip. "After the game, his parents came to check on me since their kid had knocked out my tooth. They were standing there, ready to give my folks their insurance information. They were horrified to realize no one was going to take me to see a doctor."

Any good parent would have been. She wanted to ask about his folks, but since he hadn't offered up much beyond the fact that his stepdad took off after introducing him to the motorcycle club, she thought it would be wiser to wait for him to share what he chose.

"Did they end up taking you?" Her opinion of the wealthy, jet-set Murphy family was softening.

"Yeah. And that was cool, but the best part was talking to Kyle about hockey. He was so driven and the sport was—always has been—such a science to him. He analyzed every part of his game and found ways to improve it. Other players I'd met before him were spoiled rich kids who cared more about meeting girls and soaking their parents for a new stick."

He was a million miles away as he told her that story and it was obvious the meeting had been monumental for him. Kyle had given him something to care about besides his gang brothers. Something to think about beyond what she guessed was an impoverished and dangerous childhood. The Murphy money had done some good there.

"So you became friends and they invited you back to the U.S.? Akseli Rankinen officially became Axel Rankin?" She had to admit that was a generous move. No doubt it had been a risk on their part if they knew anything about Axel's background.

"Something like that," he hedged, his fingers tightening on her waist. "It wasn't easy to accept the invitation, knowing the Destroyers might kill me before they let me out of the group. But I chose a good time to announce my decision—right after a successful beat-down that resulted in new terrain for the club. And they decided I'd be worth more to them down the road."

A knot tightened in her belly.

"Except now they expect their pound of flesh." She realized how simple and superficial her worries about her sister must sound to a man who had survived the childhood Axel had.

"I'll make sure they don't take it." He pulled her closer, pressing a warm kiss into her neck. "Don't think twice about that."

She itched to ask him more. Find out how he could fend off the group's renewed interest in him and stay safe. But he nipped her ear and tucked her hip close to his. In theory, she didn't appreciate how easily he could distract her. Yet this was their first night together. A stolen moment behind locked doors that she never wanted to end, even though three weeks from now she'd have no choice in the matter.

Just this once, she could forget about her social responsibility to noble causes and simply enjoy the night. Tomorrow would be time enough to find a way to make sure that old gang stayed far away from him. Even if she had to use the bright light of the media to chase them back to the other side of the globe.

9

"YOU DON'T LOOK ALL THAT surprised about my past."
Swiping the puck to Kyle, Axel tried to gauge his foster
brother's expression. He'd just spilled his guts about his
years with the Destroyers, culminating in the confronta-
tion with the biker on the way to the flight to Montreal.

After sleeping with Jennifer and realizing he needed
to protect her at all costs, Ax figured the time had come
to make his foster family aware of the details of his past.
While he didn't need help fighting *his* battles, it wouldn't
be fair to the Murphys to be targeted without any warning. When he'd alerted them recently about increasing
security, he'd been purposely vague. Now he needed to
reveal the truth, not just to his parents, but to his four
other brothers—Ryan, Jack, Keith and Danny.

He flipped a shot into the practice net beside Kyle—
the two of them were alone in a training room at the New
York visiting-team facility.

"Actually, I'm not." Kyle pulled a puck closer with
his stick, setting it up for his shot at the practice net

next to Axel. "You never wanted to tell us much about your background, bro, and Dad couldn't leave it up to chance."

"I don't follow." Frowning, Axel stabbed his stick into the mat and stared at his foster brother—hell, his true brother in every way that counted.

Thank God the camera guys hadn't been trailing after either of them today.

"You know Dad." Methodically, Kyle fired shot after shot, pulling a new puck into position between each goal. "He thinks research is the key to business success. He's ordered preliminary studies for every property he's ever considered buying. Do you really think he'd bring home a foreign teenager without looking into your past?"

Stunned, Axel watched as one puck after another drilled the practice net. When the last one left the goal swinging gently, he blinked away his shock.

"You knew all of it?" Axel had omitted a few of the more hellish moments, of course, figuring no one needed to know about the beat-downs he'd seen. The abused teens that showed up at the club, willing to sell their souls to be part of a new cycle of violence. One where *they* used their fists.

"Yeah." Kyle nudged Ax's stick with his. "From the start. Before we even left Helsinki that first time, Dad knew that you'd been running with those guys. But we had a family vote and it was unanimous. You were one of us, man, even then."

Axel couldn't look at his brother. Not with his freaking eyes burning and his throat dry as a desert.

"What the hell is wrong with you people?" He slammed the stick on the floor. Twice, for good measure. "I could have been a total head case. A violent lowlife who carried drugs in my suitcase."

"You didn't look like a user. And hey, you weren't so violent that I couldn't handle you. Remember how I knocked your teeth out that time?"

Axel snorted a laugh.

"Jesus. It was one tooth." He looked over at the dopey-ass, crooked-nosed brother who he loved like a son of a bitch. "I can't believe you brought me into your freaking mansion on the Cape, knowing I was some loser gangster."

"'There, but by the grace of God, go I.' I swear to you, my man, that's what Dad said when we talked about bringing you to the States. He was a roughneck before he eloped with Mom. You know her family still doesn't speak to him."

Ax could imagine Robert Murphy making that decision. The guy was a self-made billionaire, turning a clam shack into a successful restaurant and a seaside inn into a hotel conglomerate. But he hadn't started out with much of anything besides ambition and drive.

The outdated cooling system kicked on overhead, blowing a stale breeze through the workout room.

"I can't believe you've known about my history this whole time." But it would make it easier to call home ~~a~~ tell the Murphys the full extent of the potential new

"I've been in the U.S. for nine years."

"And it took us the first two just to teach you enough English that we could understand you."

"With all the curse words first on the list. I'm surprised Mom didn't kick me out after I called the first dinner horseshit."

"Luckily, she's well versed in our sense of humor."

"*You're* horseshit, man."

"Back at you, bro." Kyle flipped him a puck off the blade of his stick. "And I wouldn't worry about Mom and Dad. We can send them tickets for a Mediterranean cruise or something until this blows over."

"Right." Axel lifted his stick, rearing back to fire, then sent the puck into next year. He was rumored to have the hardest slap shot in the league this season and he meant to keep it that way. "That would help me breathe easier about them. But I can't send Jennifer away for the month. How do I keep her safe?"

"They've already seen you together?" Kyle fed him another puck.

"Yes." Ax used his stick to take out his fury, pissed that his past had caught up to him after all this time. "The biker dude looked right at her and took aim like he was going to…"

He couldn't even say the words, the image they called up was too horrific. Jennifer was a vibrant, beautiful woman, inside and out. He couldn't imagine her silenced forever. And he knew the kinds of brutality gangs could visit on a woman.

His blood chilled.

"I'd say you have two options." Kyle leaned on his stick. "One, call the cops and report the threat."

"Yeah, my old crew loves squealers. No doubt I'll wind up with my tongue cut out. But even if I didn't, it'd be a publicity nightmare. Coach Cesare will go nuts if negative press brings the team down going into the playoffs."

"Right." Kyle replaced his stick in a bin by the door. "Then your other option is to confront the local Destroyers and ask them what the hell they're doing. If they have a beef with you, they can settle up face-to-face rather than threatening your girl."

He didn't want to think about those animals coming anywhere near Jen.

"It'll still be the end of my career if I've had every bone systematically broken by pissed-off gangsters." Besides, some injuries never healed correctly. "How are you going to score any goals without me to pass to you?"

Axel put away his stick, too, and reached for his gym bag. They needed to dress for the game.

He nearly ran into Kyle, who'd stopped by the door.

"No need to worry about that since I'd obviously go in to confront these guys with you. And if they try to take you out, they'll have to go through me."

For the second time today, Kyle had knocked him on his ass in the only way he still could—metaphorically.

"That is not happening." He would go to the mat on this one. "I appreciate your willingness to have your face rearranged along with mine, but this is my fight."

"Well, then, you still haven't learned jack about your

family, have you? You have real brothers now. Not the bullshit gangster kind." Kyle didn't get angry often, but Axel could hear it in his voice now. "You don't fight alone anymore."

Unwilling to push his brother's buttons right before a game, Axel figured he'd better keep his plans to himself if he didn't want to risk a knock-down-drag-out with Kyle.

He needed to save his strength for when he faced the Destroyers.

"I know." He held out his fist, a peace offering.

He'd wanted to warn the Murphys about the possibility of violence from the motorcycle club. This conversation had taken care of that, even if Kyle hadn't liked the outcome.

Kyle bumped knuckles with him with more force than necessary. "I've got your back, Ax. Whether you want me to or not."

With a terse nod, Axel shoved open the training room door, exiting out into the visiting team's locker area.

After a 7:05 game, they'd head back to Philly, arriving shortly after midnight. One more night with Jennifer before he faced the Destroyers and found out what they wanted. Because no matter what happened, he would keep his family safe and Jennifer, too.

Even if he had to turn his back on all of them to do it.

"NEED A CLOSE-UP SHOT, Bryce." Jennifer spoke into the microphone on her headset as she watched the live feeds of the Phantoms game on six different monitors—three from stationary cameras and three manned by her crew. "We want some more emotion. Yelling, sweating, snarling."

She didn't ask just because his camera happened to be on Axel. Although, possibly, Ax's face had reminded her that she needed more tight shots. He'd been on her mind every moment since he'd left her bed this morning to get dressed for the early flight to New York. She enjoyed the chance to see him at work, his job interesting her more than she would have guessed possible given that she wasn't a sports fan. But hockey had been his ticket out of hardship, his path to a different life.

That gave her a new appreciation for the game. And she was willing to do whatever she could to see that he didn't have to give it up just because some creeps from his past started harassing him. She would research the Destroyers like an investigative reporter and search for their vulnerability—a way to hurt them with a media spotlight. But for right now, she needed to put forward solid work her boss would be proud of on the documentary.

"Will do," Bryce returned over the headset from his position along the rink.

His lens brought Axel's strong jaw into focus. The U-shaped scar on his cheek filled the frame.

"Thank you." She enjoyed the view, her hand reaching to touch his face on monitor 4. "And, Steven, can you make sure we have more footage of the guys in the box? I'd like to see their reaction to hard hits or bad calls."

"Sure thing," her most experienced technician responded. "I'm going to put one of the stationary cameras on it."

"Fine," she agreed, moving her hand off the monitor once Axel returned to the bench and another player's mug took over the screen. "And great job on the footage of Vincent Girard and his date last night, Steve."

She'd reviewed the sequence on the flight from Montreal, surprised to see the heartwarming interaction between the right winger and the groupie who didn't behave one bit like a groupie. Jennifer had learned a little about Chelsea Durant from the team's publicity person, including that she worked in the gift shop and helped out in the public relations office in her spare time. But even the publicity man, whose job it was to promote the team and be her point person on-site, wouldn't sell out the young woman about her past. Jennifer had to admit she was curious about her.

"Thanks." His terse reply suggested he knew his work was top-notch and didn't really need her approval. But then again, they'd never gotten along all that well. "Is it going to make the cut or was it a waste of my time?"

Jennifer gave in to the urge to roll her eyes since there was no one else in the makeshift editing room to see her.

"I'm not sure if we can use it since I probably need a more comprehensive waiver. I don't think Chelsea looked aware that she was on camera."

And that was an implicit part of the waiver contract for this project. The players were fair game to film at all times. But anyone else needed to be aware they were being recorded for the waiver permission to apply.

"Bullshit red tape," Steven muttered, letting all the crew know just how much he thought of her and her refusal to bend rules.

Jennifer tried to remain neutral-sounding. "I'll meet with her tonight to see if she'll sign a more comprehensive agreement to use her image."

No reply. Oh, well. She was still the boss of all the footage that she wasn't actively featured in, so she planned to protect Chelsea's wishes on this one. When Jennifer had walked into this job, she'd planned to deal fast and loose with the team to make a commercial documentary that the built-in audience of sports fans would love.

But she saw layer after layer in the narrative here, and there was a lot more going on than a winning season. The coach seemed to be reliving the career he'd lost to an injury, hell-bent on getting his team to the Stanley Cup. Leandre Archambault was trying to turn over a new leaf and find someone special, but the team pigeonholed him as a male bimbo and made it tough for him to meet the kind of woman he was looking for.

Kyle Murphy had recently become involved with a professional matchmaker whose mother was a former pop star. And, apparently the right winger was falling for the gift shop girl.

All in all, the documentary was about more than sports. It would capture a moment in time, a tough season full of gifted athletes trying to be a team in spite of the distractions. There would be something transcendent here, a human drama beneath the fierce action of the game. But Jennifer would be damned before she'd throw Chelsea Durant under the bus just to serve the commercial hook and a cameraman's ego. If she wouldn't agree to her increased role in the series, the tender footage of her squeezing Vinny Girard's hand over the dinner table would have to go.

Jen's new relationship made her more sensitive to a person's desire to protect their privacy. She just hoped she could manage the feat with Axel. An on-screen romance with him would be much more than personally awkward.

It would be downright dangerous.

A TEAM FLIGHT FROM NEW YORK to Philadelphia wouldn't have been a good spot to find privacy even on a regular day. But with two cameras rolling through the Boeing jet's main aisle, Vinny Girard figured there was little chance that any conversation with Chelsea wouldn't be overheard or recorded.

He'd have to content himself with his other small victory for the day—convincing Chelsea to take the team flight home. She'd let Misty drive her car back to Philly so her friend could stop and see some family in New York.

All around them, his teammates hammed it up for the camera crews, reenacting a particularly rough play when Axel Rankin got a penalty for slashing and the Phantoms on the ice went nuts. Vinny hadn't been skating at the time, so he felt no need to chime in. Plus it was obvious Ax wanted no part of the extra attention. Normally, the guy was as boisterous as the rest of the team, but he'd dialed it down ever since the camera crews had joined them.

"I can't believe I'm here." Chelsea sat beside Vinny in the last row of seats after another Phantoms win. They were two rows back from their nearest neighbors. "I hope it wasn't totally presumptuous of me to get on board."

She tugged at the knit cuffs of her long-sleeved shirt with the Conference Champions logo from two years ago. He'd noticed she owned almost every piece of team clothing the gift shop sold, which was probably in part because she got a discount but also because fan gear happened to be her uniform when she was on duty.

"You belong here," he reminded Chelsea, thinking about what it would be like to lean over and kiss away the worried frown from lips that were pink and plump without a trace of makeup. "Remember? The Phantoms pay your salary because you're the best team supporter we have."

Wrapping her arms around herself against the blast of cool air blowing from the overhead vents, she rolled her eyes at him.

"I think they just figured I practically lived at the rink anyhow, so why not put me to work?" She straightened as the attendant closed the plane door and asked the camera crew to have a seat. "Are we taking off?"

"Yes. Looks like we're all set." He turned down the

vent and shifted the nozzle away from her while she leaned closer for a better view over the seat rests.

For a moment, he wondered if she was a nervous flyer. Then he realized the truth.

"You've never flown before, have you?"

"Not unless you count a vicarious drug trip I took sitting beside an older woman doped up on mushrooms." She said it matter-of-factly, still watching the flight attendant prepare the cabin for takeoff. "I held her hand while she screamed that giant mosquitoes were coming to get her and described flying around on one of them."

"My God." He could picture Chelsea, unfazed and strong, talking the woman down from her high. "If I stop to think about the things you must have seen during those days…" He shook his head. "I'm sorry you had to go through that."

Chelsea turned toward him, eyes wide with genuine surprise. "I never minded nights like that. And the old lady wasn't an addict, she just had a lot of health problems and occasionally when she tried to buy something for the pain, the dealers would sell her whatever they had leftover at the end of the night." Her jaw tightened, chin lifting. "If I ever run my own shelter, I'm going to make sure my guests have access to health care. Or aspirin, at the very least."

Hearing the fierce note in her voice, Vincent reminded himself never to stand between her and the aspirin counter. What a strong advocate underprivileged people would have in someone like Chelsea. Her lean

figure and delicate features belied the drive and determination inside her.

"I think you'll find this kind of flying is less event-
ful." He wanted to take her hand and hold it this whole
trip. Feel her pulse throb under his thumb. Connect with
her in that small way that wouldn't attract attention and
wouldn't advertise a wealth of intense attraction on his
part.

Memories of the kiss he'd placed in the center of her
palm were more powerful—more sensually vivid—than
the recollections of a handful of one-night stands he'd
had since leaving his junior year in college. He'd broken
up with his high school girlfriend that year, a girl from
back home who'd never understood his need to pursue
his dream of playing hockey.

He'd learned then that love didn't grow when you stifled each other, which was why he was going to try not
to push Chelsea for too much, too soon.

Now, as the plane picked up speed on the runway, he
looked over at her in the seat beside him. She gripped
the armrests with both hands, her shoulders tense. Her
cheeks seemed pale as she worried her lower lip, yet
she'd never told him she was nervous. Never let on the
idea of flying scared her.

That's when he knew, ready or not, he had to touch
her.

"Hold my hand," he told her by way of warning, sliding his fingers under her forearm to pry her loose from
the armrest. "It'll be easier."

She didn't say anything one way or the other, but she locked gazes with him for a moment. Nodded.

His heartbeat stuttered for a second as he took her left hand in his and—God help him—wrapped his right arm around her shoulders. She thought she was scared of takeoff?

She'd know exactly how terrified he was of scaring her off when she got a load of his heart banging the hell out of his chest where she settled her cheek. The scent of her hair wafted up, teasing him with something clean and floral.

After months of watching her and wanting her, having her curled against him felt better than a winning season. His last girlfriend had given him an ultimatum—hockey or her. And Vinny had chosen to pursue his dream.

But right now, with Chelsea in his arms, he knew he could set down his stick and not think twice about it. She was it for him. The One. He liked everything about her, from how easily she loaned her car to a friend to how she pulled people into her circle, from homeless women to hockey players. She had a natural warmth that people gravitated toward.

Him included.

He would have been content to spend the whole flight home like that. No, more than that, he would have felt privileged to touch her that whole time.

But they'd barely leveled out at flying altitude when the director lady made her way down the aisle, her eye on the two of them. Her red curls fought a ponytail, with kinky pieces sliding free along her cheek. She held a clipboard under her arm, a large silver bracelet clanking against it with each step. A sense of foreboding clanged nearer along with her.

Vinny couldn't have said why he felt like trouble was on the way, beyond the fact that a visitor would surely make Chelsea sit up and let go of his hand. But he did.

"Hi!" Jennifer Hunter slid into the seat beside him, her long skirt brushing his knee as it swirled to settle after her. "So sorry to bother you, but I wanted to speak to you both about the series."

Chelsea must have heard her despite the engine noise, which was loudest in these seats at the back of the plane. Releasing his hand, she straightened.

"It's no bother," Chelsea assured the other woman while Vinny mentally disagreed vigorously.

His body had memorized the feel of Chelsea's already. The sensation of her against him would remain imprinted on his skin for days. Months. Maybe forever. He sure as hell hadn't been ready for it to end.

"Great." Jennifer set the clipboard on her lap and leaned closer. "I've got some footage of the two of you I'd love to use in this week's show, but it was filmed at a distance. And while our agreement with the team covers that kind of shot, I wanted to make sure Chelsea felt comfortable with it."

Beside him, Chelsea tensed. He could sense it without even looking at her. That's how in tune he was to this woman.

"What kind of footage?" he barked, the surly note

totally out of character for him, but damn it, he felt protective.

"I can show you on my laptop." She spoke to Chelsea, looking right past him. "There's a snippet of you two talking after the game in Montreal, and since that was on the ice, it's well within our right to use. However, there's a scene of the two of you having dinner—"

"No." Incensed, he could only imagine how Chelsea would feel to have her privacy invaded like that. "Absolutely not."

"I'd like to see it," Chelsea said, her hand coming to rest on his knee as if to placate him.

Quiet the beast.

It worked like a charm since he was stunned silent. He could hardly believe his luck after all these months of trying to get her alone. Chelsea didn't ever date, that he saw. She admitted to issues with men, a fact that made him feel slightly homicidal toward whatever guy had scared her.

Yet Chelsea had reached out to him. Touched him. Come into his arms willingly today. Things were looking up, except that she seemed ready to sacrifice her privacy for the sake of the documentary. Why would she give permission for the camera crew to broadcast a private moment between them?

"Great." Jennifer stood, her long, cherry-colored skirt catching on the armrest until she yanked it off. "Would you like to come up front with me to watch the clip?"

"Sure." Chelsea rose carefully, watchful of the overhead compartment that was low next to the window seat. "I'll be there in a minute."

"Take your time," the director urged, bracelet clanking as she walked away.

"You don't have to do this," Vincent assured Chelsea once the filmmaker was several rows away from them.

"I know." She tried to slip past him into the aisle, but he stood up so she would have more room.

He was prepared to take his time with her, but he didn't think his long-suffering libido would handle those kinds of tight quarters.

"I think you can just refuse, don't you?" He kept his voice low, even though the other guys were still revved up from the game, the noise level high. "Otherwise, she wouldn't have asked, she would have just used the footage."

"I agree." She flipped a dark brown wave out of one eye. "But last night. That dinner we had together. It was one of the best things that has ever happened to me. I wouldn't mind reliving it."

Before he could yank his jaw off the floor, she sauntered her way up the aisle, her gorgeous figure hidden in loose-fitting jeans that didn't attract any particular attention, thank God. Though his teammates knew better than to hit on her.

But he, in the meantime, was apparently one of the best things to ever happen to her. Hunger for Chelsea surging to an all-time high, Vinny decided he was going to up his game.

Tonight.

10

"I HATE PLAYING GAMES for the cameras," Axel growled in Jennifer's ear, the clear cell phone connection making it feel as if he was there in the car with her instead of driving his own vehicle ahead of her. "I wanted to catch hold of that long skirt you were wearing on the plane and use it to pull you closer to me when you were marching through the cabin like you owned the place."

Tucking the earpiece tighter to her ear, Jennifer smiled as she followed the taillights on Ax's big black Escalade through the Philadelphia suburbs toward his house. Heat warmed her chest, sending pleasant sensations all over her body. How on earth was she going to go back to New York as if none of this ever happened? She knew a relationship with a hockey star would not be the right life for her. She had her own goals and dreams, and they didn't involve following around a world-famous athlete. Still, she couldn't imagine walking away.

"You couldn't have done that even if there were no cameras," she chided, thinking how much she would have liked falling into his lap. "Unless you've got exhibitionist tendencies."

"You'd be surprised what I could do to you very discreetly in a seat on a plane."

Jennifer nearly missed the turn he'd taken, distracted by the idea.

"How perfectly shocking." She tried to sound scandalized, but wound up sounding breathless and sex-starved.

"They give out blankets if you ask for them, you know." He put on his signal light well in advance of the next turn.

The houses kept getting bigger in this part of town, the streets lined with honest-to-goodness mansions, the manicured lawns illuminated by extensive landscape lighting.

"And why would you need a blanket? Does the idea of being with me make you sleepy?" she teased, hoping his house was close.

She'd wanted him since the moment she'd rolled out of bed with him this morning. Watching him play via close-up shots, seeing his passion and intensity channeled into the game, had only made her want him more.

"I'd need a blanket to hide the fact that I would have had my hand under your skirt."

"Shameless," she chastised, practically drooling. She shifted in her seat to ward off the ache for him, but that only intensified the heat.

"For the sake of touching you? Absolutely."

Her heart pounded so hard she felt light-headed.

"Can I ask you a question?" She slowed for a speed bump beside a Tudor mansion that looked as though an English king ought to be living there.

"Does it involve specific sexual requests? Because I can already say yes."

She licked her lips, distracted by the possibilities. A perfectly honed athlete to fulfill her every sensual fantasy.

"Um. Actually, no. But I'd like to get back to that offer."

Ax's Escalade turned into a driveway and she realized the long, looping horseshoe drive was for the Tudor mansion.

Holy crap. He lived here?

"I'm ready." His voice was a masculine rumble in her ear, prompting her out of her goggle-eyed appraisal of the multimillion-dollar property.

She followed him toward a converted carriage house in the back where an overhead door opened and light flooded onto the lawn. Two pristine sports cars sat inside the glorified garage, the floor so neat it could have been a showroom. Jennifer shoved her rental into Park and turned off the engine.

"I just wondered. What do you think causes sexual chemistry to come barreling out of the blue?" She pocketed the car keys while he got out of his vehicle.

"Just a sec," he answered, disconnecting the phone call as he jogged back to open her door. Then, offering his hand to help her out, he continued, "That sounded like a question that needed a personal answer."

Gazing up at him, she visualized him in a slow-motion shot that would capture him the way she saw him now. All hard angles and intensity, a brooding heat in his eyes even as he dusted off the chivalrous manners to draw her to her feet. He closed the door behind her and folded her hand onto his forearm as he guided her across the driveway to the sidewalk.

"I don't know why I asked." Nervousness tingled over her and she felt out of her depth with him suddenly. It was one thing to tease and flirt with a Neanderthal hockey player trying to intimidate her with the scent of sweat. It was another to sleep with a wealthy athlete who traveled the world acquiring exotic cars. "I guess I just wondered why this hit us so hard when we don't really have much in common."

Winding around some wrought-iron patio furniture, he took her to a back door entrance where he keyed in a code to disarm the security system. More exterior lights clicked on, revealing an outdoor living area under a covered pergola, complete with easy chairs and a huge television screen against one wall, protected by a clear plastic casing. Outside the man cave, a multilevel pool beckoned despite the cooler spring temperatures.

"I have a great answer to this." Opening the door, he flipped on lights in an expansive kitchen and dining area with lots of white tile and windows overlooking the backyard.

"Really?" She still half expected him to give her some outrageously flirtatious response to distract her completely. But she was curious about the immediate connection she'd felt to him, a draw she knew he'd felt, too.

"I think sexual chemistry is nature's wake-up call." He set his keys on a long kitchen table that looked like a reclaimed door from a turn-of-the-century home. He must have left his travel bag in the car because he hadn't brought it inside.

"How so?" She ditched her purse beside his keys and toed off a pair of worn ballet flats. There was no need to pretend she wasn't spending the night when she'd been daydreaming about him for hours.

"It's a cosmic alarm system that tells you to pay attention to someone you might miss out on otherwise." He reached up to twine a finger through one of her curls, winding it loosely around his knuckle before he let it slide free again. "Think about it. If we were only attracted to the people who made for the most logical partners—ones who shared all our interests and thought like we do—life would be pretty boring."

"So sexual chemistry leads us into crazy relationships that could never work in the real world." She shivered in the wake of his touch and tried not to be disappointed that his answer had brought him to the same conclusion as her.

"That's not it at all." He tipped her chin up, meeting her gaze. His sea-blue eyes seemed to peer deep inside her. "All that hot attraction helps us find people who challenge us. People who have the potential to make us better. I learned a long time ago that taking the easy path isn't always a smart idea. Sometimes you need to try the unexpected."

"Like a gangster biker turning into a hockey star?" She could see where he'd taken a huge risk to break out of his old life.

"More like a nice, normal hockey player getting the hots for a social crusader with a fiery temper and killer bod." His thumb traced a trail down her cheek, tantalizing her.

Warm pleasure curled inside her and she wanted to hug the feeling to her chest, savor it close and not let it go. Because this wasn't just physical pleasure. His words made her feel…special.

"My temper is overrated," she argued softly, her cheek tipping toward his hand to increase the pressure of that light, glancing touch.

"But you have a fiery side," he pressed, stepping closer until he stood a mere inch away from her. "And I'm going to prove it to you all over again in just a few minutes."

Longing swept through her, a sweet layer of sensual awareness over the tenderness she felt for him.

She was falling for him.

The realization made her want to catch herself, like a child who changes his mind about going down the slide at the last minute. But then his lips found hers in a gentle caress, moving over her mouth with infinite care and thoroughness. That sexual chemistry flamed hot and carnal, a flash fire that burned away her hesitation and reminded her how much she wanted him.

Until all she could think about was him.

She could only hope that he felt the same.

SELFISH. BASTARD.

Axel could think of no better words to describe himself as he allowed himself to touch Jennifer all over again. He'd wanted one more night with her, one more time to savor everything about her before he backed off to keep her safe while he dealt with the Destroyers.

Yet the more he got to know her, the more selfish that seemed. And the tougher it would be to let her go.

Now, lifting her up, he held her at the perfect height to taste her. Her toes dangled against his shins, her body soft and yielding. She kissed with abandon, her tongue stroking his in a way that turned him inside out.

"Can we take this upstairs?" He broke away long enough to see her nod, then set her on her feet. "Follow me."

"Your house is beautiful," she murmured, smoothing a hand over a long buffet table in a hallway.

"I was lucky to snag it from the guy I was traded for. It's big enough to have company." He knew the place was probably ostentatious in her eyes. She had a vaguely bohemian-hippie vibe with her passion for art with a cause. But damn it, he'd worked hard for what he had. "I like having people over."

"Teammates? Or is that a nosy question?"

"Not at all. And yeah, it's good to get the team together. There aren't many of us who drink during the season, so why go to a bar? It's more fun to hang out at someone's house. Watch games. Play billiards. Stuff like that." He'd appreciated that about life in the Murphy house. Always some brothers around to shoot hoops or throw darts.

"Like a gang without the violence." She lifted the hem of her long skirt as she went up the stairs.

He couldn't remember ever finding a glimpse of ankle so freaking sexy before. But the sight of her bare feet and pink toenails on his wool carpet runner turned him on something fierce.

"Kind of." He hadn't really looked at his team that way, but maybe he had traded one brotherhood for another. "Hockey players can brawl with the best of them."

"Kyle, for instance." She paused at the top of the steps, peering around the long hallway full of doors.

"You give him too much credit," he grumbled, waving her toward the master suite, dying to touch more of her as he flicked on the lights. "One good punch and you're making him out to be Muhammad Ali. You really should meet my whole family one of these days—"

He broke off, realizing that she wouldn't be meeting the Murphys. Not if the Destroyers were serious about coming after him since he would need to make it look as though she was out of his life for good.

If she detected his abrupt departure from the topic, she didn't show it. In fact, she seemed to shy away from the idea, too.

"Maybe I will," she murmured vaguely, stepping into his room where a king-size bed rested beside a wall of windows and French doors led out to a balcony overlooking the pool. "For now, I'm mostly interested in seeing more of you."

"I like how you think, Jen." He reached for her, bunching a handful of the fabric from her long skirt in his hand and pulling her closer. "I've been waiting for the chance to touch you all day."

The thin cotton tightened around her legs as he reeled her in, making him realize she had another layer beneath it. Some kind of satiny slip.

"That's good because I've been on edge ever since that conversation in the car on the way over here."

He remembered telling her he wished he could have touched her on the plane. Hidden the contact under a blanket.

"Remind me to whisper suggestive scenarios to you more often." Letting go of her skirt, he let the fabric flow over his hand as he palmed the tight curve of her butt through the slip.

Massaging her through the silky material, he felt the outline of her panties. A thong with a barely there T-back. Possibly a little bow or a rosette that perched high between her cheeks at the small of her back.

"I don't think that's a good idea," she cautioned, her eyelids falling to half mast as he touched her. "I'm highly suggestible."

"Meaning I can talk you into naughty things?"

"Meaning you shouldn't try." She lifted her fingers to the buttons on her blouse and began to work on them.

Eyes glued to the creamy skin she revealed, the scrap of yellow lace that cupped her breasts the way he wanted to, Axel dragged in a steadying breath. He wanted to make this last for her and he couldn't do that if he kept fantasizing about her. He needed her to be the one fantasizing about him.

"I can get the buttons," he assured her, releasing her delectable rump to handle the blouse.

"No." She kept a tight grip on the buttons. "I love what you were doing."

He hid a smile at that bossy side that had no problem telling him what to do. Instead, he skimmed a touch up the backs of her thighs, liking the little sigh she made when he hit the curve of her bottom.

An erogenous zone.

How fortunate for both of them that he'd located a sweet spot. He made plans to revisit it again and again, but for now, he watched her breasts strain at the skimpy lace bra she wore, her nipples tightening into dark shadows he could see beneath the material.

"Ax." She had her blouse twisted around her hands behind her, her wrists stuck in the narrow sleeves. "I don't think I can go slow tonight."

"That's why your hands are caught," he chastised, smiling as he reached to help her. "Too much of a hurry."

His chest grazed her breasts as he leaned against her, the beaded flesh the sweetest abrasion through the lace.

"That's not my fault when the foreplay started in the car." She wriggled enticingly, no doubt trying to break his concentration.

And doing a damn thorough job of it.

"I thought women liked foreplay." He unfastened the

cuffs of her sleeves, which she'd forgotten to undo, freeing her.

"We also like delivery of the goods." She wrestled out of her bra straps and popped the front clasp before she rubbed her breasts against his chest.

Heat flared all over his skin, wreaking havoc with his control.

"I wanted to be so good to you," he growled in her ear, knowing she was going to win this battle.

"You can be so good to me while you're inside me," she urged, her hips nudging against his, cradling his erection. "Can't you?"

The scent of lilies of the valley and potent, sexy female—made him hungry for her. He wanted to feel her, lick her, hear her moans as she came for him over and over again.

"Yes." He lifted her off her feet and carried her to his bed, dropping her in the middle of the white comforter. "Just as soon as I get a taste of you."

He left her skirt and the slip on, shoving the fabric up and away until only her panties stood between him and what he wanted. The thong was so insubstantial he didn't bother taking it off, merely peeled the damp lace aside to take her in his mouth.

Her gasp turned into breathy sighs and soft pleas until her hips twisted against him. He spread her thighs wider, licking deeper, savoring every last drop of her slick heat. When her back arched, he wasn't ready for it to end. Could have feasted on her all day. But she came apart for him so sweetly that he couldn't make her wait any longer.

He leaned away from her as the aftershocks subsided, shedding his clothes and finding a condom. Her eyes followed him, dark and smoldering, all that female sensuality just waiting for him.

The thought made his cock twitch, the need to be inside her so strong that sweat broke out along his brow. Sitting on the edge of the bed, he lifted her so that she straddled him, her knees hugging his hips as she looped her arms around his neck. Kissed him.

Before he could position himself where he wanted, she reached between them to stroke his hard length. Traced a circle around the tip with her thumb. While he was still seeing stars behind his eyelids, she lifted up on her toes to hover over him, then lowered herself on him. Taking him inside that soft, wet heat.

He couldn't breathe. Couldn't slow things down. He could only squeeze her hips tight, dragging her closer. When he was able to wrench his eyes open again, her small breasts swayed close enough for him to take one in his mouth. Roll one tight nipple between his teeth.

She pumped her hips faster, harder. Her hands clutched his shoulders, his arms, his chest. She whispered his name in his ear, going still for a long moment before another release claimed her, ravishing her body, teasing wave after wave of fulfillment from her.

Axel held her closer, pushing inside her again to coax one last sweet spasm, when his own climax blindsided him. He came hard and long until he was damn near breathless, his legs spent and his body totally sated.

He wanted to pause the night right there. Make sure the sun didn't rise for another seventy-two hours or so in order for him to get his fill of this woman. Then again, that would never be enough. Last night hadn't begun to take the edge off his need today. If anything, being with her yesterday had only made the hunger sharper.

Rolling Jennifer to her side, he held her close in his bed, the lights still bright in the room even though it was long past 1:00 a.m. He was lucky to have any juice in him after the game against New York. Actually, she was the reason he'd had any energy at all. But it caught up to him now—the game, the incredible sex.

Exhaustion crept over him even as he pulled the covers tighter around Jen and smoothed her hair from her cheek to make her more comfortable. He couldn't stop the morning from coming. And he had to find a way to protect her from his old gang.

But letting go of her now?

He might as well go out and tilt at a few windmills and rope the moon while he was at it.

11

"I'M TAKING YOU HOME."

Vincent's words pierced through any lingering sleepiness from the snooze Chelsea had grabbed on the flight from New York. They'd been the last ones off the plane since she'd fallen asleep on Vinny's shoulder. Now, the cool night air and the startling idea of going back to her place with a man had her instantly alert.

She peered out into the small parking lot of the private airfield, the other players hopping into expensive cars and making tracks for home.

"That's okay," she said reflexively, "I can drive…"

Belatedly, she recalled that Misty had her car. Chelsea hadn't thought about a ride from the airport when she'd agreed to take the flight to Philadelphia with the team.

"I'm happy to call you a cab," Vincent assured her, patient and low-key as he dropped their bags to the curb. "But you'll be home a lot faster if I drive."

He took out his cell while her nervousness evaporated.

"You're right. It's okay." She raked her hands through her hair and wished she was normal. The kind of woman who didn't freak out over small stuff like the offer of a ride from a perfectly nice guy. Actually, a really hot nice guy. "I trust you."

"You sure?" He kept the phone in his hand, hazel eyes more brown than green tonight in the buzzing fluorescent lamp high above them. "Not about trusting me. I mean about the ride."

His sheepish grin made her smile, too. Where did he get that ability to put her so at ease? Maybe it came from being around him for months. She'd seen him nearly every day—except when the team had gone on long road trips—since September.

"I'm certain about both." She reached for her duffel to lug it to his car, but seeing her intent, he grabbed the handle first.

"Great, but I carry all bags." He looped the straps of both bags over his shoulder and gestured toward the first row of the small parking lot. "I'm right over here."

In that gentlemanly way, he opened the passenger door of his heavy-duty truck, which looked as if it would be at home on a Minnesota farm—except that it was brand-spanking-new. He stowed the bags and slid into the driver's seat. All the while she played back their conversation in the restaurant the other night. He'd asked her to have dinner with him tomorrow. No. Now that it was almost one in the morning, technically they'd be seeing each other again later today.

He turned on the ignition and country music blared out surround-sound speakers. He hurried to lower the volume.

"Whoops. Must have been rocking out when I pulled in here yesterday." He shifted into Drive and stared at her in the light of the illuminated parking lot. "Where to?"

She rattled off the address with more than a little pride. "It's just an apartment, but it took me a while to get on my feet enough to make regular rent payments so...I love it. Just thinking about my very own place can still get me choked up."

Now that she had a home, she was at least normal in that way. She didn't take it for granted for a minute.

"Damn." He steered the truck out onto the access road, turning the heater on low as the temperature had dropped. "That must have been a great feeling."

"It was. Even better than when I bought my SUV." She tucked her toes under the heating vent beneath the dashboard and savored the scent of the new leather seats.

The scents of "new" and "clean" were personal aphrodisiacs even after all this time since those homeless days. Then again, maybe the memory of waking up on Vinny's shoulder had something to do with the warm simmer of blood in her veins.

"How'd you do it, Chels? If you don't mind me asking. How did you turn that corner from not having a home to—" he gestured toward her, an appreciative smile on his face "—to walking into the Phantoms' practice rink and making half the team fall in love with you?"

"Oh, please." She waved away the over-the-top flattery. "Your teammates always love the women who don't proposition them before even saying hello. It's part of the irony of being an athlete, isn't it? Tough to find romance when women expect you to be…you know…sexual gods, or something."

Vinny coughed—choked really—so that she thought she might have to pound him on the back.

"I plead the Fifth on that one. I withdraw the comment, in fact." He clutched his chest as though he was still finding it hard to breathe and when his gaze came her way again, there was an electric awareness in them that made her shift in her seat.

"That's okay." She wondered if she'd been too forward to make such a racy remark. She honestly had no idea how to behave around a guy she liked. "I'm glad you asked about what turned things around for me. When most people hear that I've been homeless, they just change the subject as fast as possible."

His forearm flexed as he turned the steering wheel, driving toward her apartment under the glow of streetlamps and a few all-night restaurants. Of course, it didn't take much movement to flex muscle on Vinny. He was incredibly strong. Perfectly made. Self-conscious about where her thoughts were leading, Chelsea felt her cheeks heat.

"I'm sure they're curious about how you put it behind

you, too. Maybe most people don't feel like they know you well enough to ask."

Whereas Vinny did. Her heart warmed inside her and it didn't have anything to do with the heat blowing out of the vents.

"Basically, I researched where to shower, where to find free clothes and where to nab easy jobs that paid by the day. I didn't take money from the government because I was seventeen when I left home and the last thing I wanted was to be thrown into the foster care system."

"When you say 'research,' what do you mean?" He turned onto her street, slowing as he approached her apartment building. "You asked around?"

"No. I went to the library and looked up gyms. I made a few fake membership badges." She glanced his way to gauge his reaction. "It was dishonest, but you have no idea how well it worked to keep some of my stuff in gym lockers around the city. And obviously, the hot showers were a huge perk."

"Clever." He pulled the truck into a space in front of her building. "But I'm surprised storage was such an issue. You couldn't just lock stuff up in a bus depot locker?"

"They're not safe." She shivered, trying not to think about some of her encounters in places like bus depots. "Airports are cleaner and more secure, but only because they police them better. Which means you can't sleep there very long. But any place that lets homeless people snooze for hours at a time is going to attract crime."

He shut off the engine, his eyes seeing too much as he studied her across the truck cab.

"Okay. So you researched to find the safe, clean places. You worked whenever you could. What else?" He turned in his seat, giving her his undivided attention.

She couldn't remember anyone ever looking at her the way he did. As if he wanted to know everything about her and would wait as long as it took to find out. Some long latent dreams stirred to life as she stared back into his hazel eyes.

"I, uh…" She forced herself to stick to the subject and not be too forward. No more uncensored comments, like calling him a sex god, damn it. "I tried to be patient and persistent. It's impossible to get ahead very quickly because when you're on the streets you're so far behind it's overwhelming to think about acquiring everything you need to build a life again. So you can't dwell on it. You just have to take small steps toward it. Build your resources slowly and try to stay healthy and safe."

Her last word seemed to echo in the truck cab. But maybe it was just her ears. Her perspective. Safety had consumed her thoughts every second she wasn't working at a job to get ahead.

Outside the truck, the nighttime residents of the streets claimed their territory. An old man pushing a grocery cart, his layers of clothes flapping around him like bat wings. A middle-aged woman in a short skirt and ripped stockings, probably between clients, as she plied her dangerous trade. A teenager who walked as if he owned the city strode past them both, flicking a discarded cigarette on the old man as he brushed past.

"I wish I'd been there to protect you." Vinny's words called her back from the scene outside.

"Me, too," she whispered, blindly reaching for his hand as she met his gaze. "I like being here with you. No one hurt me—you know, *seriously* hurt me. But I woke up once with a knee in my back and—"

She hesitated.

"You don't have to tell me if you're not ready." He closed his fingers around her hand, his warmth filtering through to her, enveloping her.

"It was a long time ago." Besides, she trusted Vinny. "I made the mistake of sleeping in an alley in a good neighborhood. I'd cased it for days, checking out what kind of people went through there at night and it seemed quiet. But the first time I let myself fall asleep there, I got jumped by some rich kid who'd come home late and high as a kite."

Vinny swallowed hard and tried not to let his anger show in his eyes. Because he would have gutted the guy if he'd been there. But obviously, no one would have ever tried to touch Chelsea if he'd been there in the first place.

It was more important that he be here for her in this moment, reassuring her tonight rather than wishing he'd been there to protect her in the past.

"Thank God you got away." He owed the Almighty big-time for that one, and he wouldn't forget to pay back.

He double-checked the lots to make sure he was

taking good care of Chelsea. Thankfully, tinted windows gave them some privacy from the handful of people who'd drifted past the vehicle.

"I lost a year's worth of savings in the knapsack I left behind, but I was fast and I fought dirty. I don't think I would have escaped if I hadn't scoped the place out for so long ahead of time, but I found my way around in the dark." She took a deep breath and flexed her fingers between his, squeezing. "I hid in a neighbor's pool house until the guy got tired of shouting for me and lights started popping on around the neighborhood."

"Damn." He shook his head, glad he'd been able to hold back worse curses. "You must have been so scared. I'm all tense just listening to you tell me about it." Partly because he itched to strangle any man who would lift a hand to her. "Would it be okay if I held you? I don't know if it would help you, but after hearing that, it would sure as hell help *me* feel better."

Her hand still squeezed his, but she nodded.

Relief shot through him because he wasn't lying. He needed to have his arms around her. Reassure himself she was okay.

Untwining his fingers from hers, he slid closer to her on the big bench seat. But before he could slip an arm behind her shoulders, she ducked her head to his chest and looped her hands around his waist, relaxing against him.

He realized then that he hadn't exhaled since she'd started her story. Only now could he let out his breath. Resting his chin on top of her head, he stroked her back.

"I'm so glad you fought dirty," he whispered. "And that you were so much smarter than that piece of crap who came after you. Because I don't know what I would have done this year without you, Chelsea."

She stirred, edging back to peer up at him in the cab.

"What are you talking about?" Her brow crinkled in confusion.

"Looking forward to seeing you every day—that's what got me through the first half of this season when I was playing like crap and the hockey bloggers all said I should pack my bags and go home." He smoothed a thumb over the creamy softness of her cheek. "I didn't settle in with the team right away, but you were always there in the stands, cheering me on. I figured I'd stick with it long enough for a chance to ask you out."

"Thank goodness it took you a long time to ask me because now you're playing like a super stud." She blinked up at him from under her long bangs, her lips so full and kissable that he had to take deep breaths to rein himself in.

No way would he scare her off by moving too fast.

"By now, they'll have to throw me out of Philadelphia to get me to leave." In fact, he wasn't sure how he'd be able to let her walk into that apartment building without him. She felt so good in his arms. So right.

"But what if I want to see Minnesota sometime?" she asked, surprising him.

Did she know how badly he wanted a future with her? How much it would mean to him to be able to take her home?

"You've got a ride to Cloquet right here." He patted the truck's dashboard, then returned his hand to her waist, careful to stay closer to her rib cage than the subtle swell of her hip.

She'd told him she'd been patient during those years on the streets. So he'd damn well be patient however long it took for her to let him touch her the way he wanted.

"Vinny?"

"Yeah?"

"I think I'd like cows."

"You do?" He grinned and felt her snag another piece of his heart.

"They sound very nonjudgmental." She reached toward him, her hand alighting on his chest, right above his heart.

She'd never taken the initiative to touch him before, since he didn't count her falling asleep on him during the flight home. So having her fingers sketch ever so softly along his shirt seemed like the hottest foreplay he'd ever known.

"I don't know if I can get back to introduce you to them until the season's over." He tried to focus on the conversation instead of how good it felt to have her hand on him. "But if I can't bring you to Cloquet, I can bring a little Cloquet to you. My parents are coming to town next week. Maybe you can meet them."

His first clue that he'd done something wrong came when her touch evaporated like dew on a hot day. In an instant, she retreated in so many ways his brain could barely calculate them all, but her shuttered gaze was the one that spoke the loudest.

"Your parents?"

He realized she edged backward on the seat so that he'd have to stretch if he wanted to keep his hands on her. Carefully, he released her and tried to soothe her worries.

"Yes. I sent them tickets for our first home game in the playoffs. They'll only be here for three days, but maybe we could have dinner together."

She'd already agreed to dinner with him tonight, after all. And he hadn't even asked to come upstairs with her, so it wasn't as if he was pushing any kind of physical relationship. Still, she'd backed up so much she bumped the power-lock button with her elbow.

"I don't know. Maybe." She gave him a halfhearted smile. "I'm sorry, but I didn't realize how late it was and I have to work at the gift shop tomorrow. I really should—"

"Wait." What had he done wrong? "I don't want to pressure you—"

"You're not," she assured him, snagging her purse and levering open the door.

"I want to at least walk you into the building." He reached out to keep her there.

She tensed at his touch.

"I'm sorry. I have to go." She fumbled for her keys.

He hopped out of the driver's-side door and came around, but she was already at the entrance to her building.

"Chelsea, what's wrong?" He didn't want to hold her there, knowing she had issues with being touched.

God knows, he would never restrain her if she wanted to leave, but she was backing away from him so fast she'd never even hear him if he didn't get closer.

"I'm sorry." She shook her head, flipping her key upside down to try it in the lock the other way. "I don't know what I'm doing and I can't…I just can't do this."

For a minute he thought she meant she couldn't open her lock. But then she had the lock open and stepped inside, holding the door half-shut to talk to him through a slit as if he was some kind of criminal.

"I'm sorry, Vinny." Her voice cracked as she squeezed the door in a white-knuckled grip. "You deserve a nice, normal girl. And that will never be me."

THE FIRST INSTALLMENT of the documentary series would debut on television tonight.

Jennifer had to leave Ax's place at dawn to put in some overtime hours editing footage from the game and the team's plane ride home the night before. She'd see Axel at the practice rink in a couple of hours, but when she'd left his house, he'd still been sleeping. Now, arriving at her temporary office, she peered over her shoulder, certain she'd heard someone behind her. But all seemed quiet.

The morning was still cool as she shoved through the double doors to the conference room, surprised to discover no one else from the crew had reported to work yet. Maybe they'd opted to work late into the night instead.

While she poured water into the coffeemaker, hoping some caffeine would wake her up, her cell phone rang. She set down the carafe and looked at her phone, noticing her sister's number on her caller ID.

"Hey, Julia," she answered. "What are you doing awake at the crack of dawn?"

Her gaze went to the photo she'd brought from home, a picture of the two of them shopping for a Christmas tree on a road trip to the country last winter. They had their arms slung around each other's shoulders, goofy knit hats dotted with snow.

"It's a school day," her sister groused, sounding as if she hadn't had her morning coffee, either. Or whatever it was that fifteen-year-old girls needed in the a.m. to take the edge off. Some days Jennifer felt as if she'd been born decades older than anyone else in her family. "I have no choice."

"Oh. Right." Jennifer searched the drawers for a plastic spoon to measure the coffee. "How has school been?"

Julia had switched to a new school over the holidays and the transition had been bumpy. Their mother had never been very involved in either of their lives so Jennifer had made it her mission to ensure Julia could escape the drama of that awful fall semester. Jennifer had paid the tuition, arranged for transportation and bought the wardrobe, wanting to ensure Julia felt taken care of.

"I hate it. I want to go back with my friends."

Jennifer spilled the coffee she'd been trying to measure.

"You're kidding." She set down the spoon and turned her back on the cabinet to focus on the conversation.

"No. That's why I called. I asked the principal if you can get a refund on the tuition for this semester and he said no. But I'm willing to work a part-time job to pay you back."

"I don't want the money back." She couldn't believe her ears. "I want you to attend a school where you'll be happy. Where you don't have people whispering behind your back."

A sound outside the conference room startled her and a shadow passed by one of the frosted-glass windows. She hoped it was someone from her camera crew.

"I'm not worried about that, Jen. I know you would have liked to attend a school like this, but it's not for me."

"You were miserable," Jen reminded her sister. "Mortified." How could Julia suggest that Jennifer had helped her transfer for selfish reasons?

"But I'm over it," Julia huffed. "And the rest of the class probably would've moved on to some new drama by the time we came back from the holidays, but we— that is, *I*—freaked out and left school."

"Julia." Jennifer sat down at the conference-room table, determined to talk some sense into her sister. She straightened the photo of her with Julia—her sister's freckles circled both cheeks like cinnamon on an apple. "This is your future we're talking about. How can you earn good grades with the distraction of online gossip and negative cliques using social media to wage a smear campaign?"

"I don't think it's that bad."

"Not that bad? I have a film project in the works to spotlight the dangers of—"

"Stop. Stop right there." Her sister's voice rose on the other end of the line, squeaking in a panicky note that only a teen could manage. "I am not going to be one of your causes. You have no right to turn your camera on my life. This is private."

"It wouldn't be about you," she clarified. "But I've heard stories about—"

"I don't care. You can go make movies about the five million other problems in the world, but not this one. Not mine." In the background, a horn sounded and her sister sighed. "My ride is here. I have to go. But, Jen, I am not a crisis you have to fix, okay? I love you. And if you love me, you'll let this go."

"But—" The call disconnected before she could argue, leaving her frustrated.

Since when had a good sisterly deed become such an annoyance? She didn't see Julia as a cause. She'd simply felt her sister's hurt and wanted to fix it.

"Knock, knock?" A woman's voice at the door startled her.

Turning, she saw Chelsea Durant in the open entry to the conference room, a coffee mug in hand. That must have been who she'd seen out the window. Why was Jen so jumpy today?

"Sorry to bother you." Chelsea lifted the ceramic mug. "I was in search of java and thought I'd see if anyone started the pot yet."

Her eyes shifted to the spilled grounds on the counter and the open bag sagging against the empty carafe.

"I got a phone call in the middle of starting it," Jennifer explained, rising. "But I think I'm going to add about ten more cups to my original estimate."

"I'm having one of those days, too," Chelsea informed her, entering the room with a surprisingly silent step. "I can make it for us."

She reached the counter before Jennifer did, so Jen let the other woman take over. The he-man aura of the Phantoms' conference room meant an abundance of black countertops and a coffee station with lots of real sugar and not nearly enough low-calorie substitutes. Jennifer had been having a tough time finding everything she needed anyhow, and Chelsea seemed to know her way around every part of the mammoth practice facility.

"We didn't get much sleep last night, did we?" Jennifer observed, wishing that was the reason for her sudden exhaustion when it had more to do with Julia's teenage psychoanalysis and the dangerous game Axel played with his old gang.

"No." Chelsea rolled up the sleeves of her Phantoms jersey and measured more water. "But I also didn't sleep because Vinny and I… There was a misunderstanding. I don't think we're going to be much of a story for your documentary."

"You're kidding." Jen had thought that was a go for sure. "I have to say, I'm a pretty good judge of emotions after watching people through a camera lens for so many years." Although possibly she wasn't as good reading people in real life since she'd gotten her sister all wrong. "And I really thought there was something special between you two."

"I know." Chelsea pressed Start on the coffee machine and turned to face Jen. "I thought so, too. But I've got no business being with a guy like him."

"How can you say that?" She didn't know Chelsea well, but Axel seemed to think she was a good person who'd had a tough life. And given how much Axel knew about hardship, Jennifer trusted his assessment. "You deserve happiness as much as anyone else."

"Maybe." Chelsea shrugged. "But what if you can't find a way through the obstacles to reach that happiness? What if there are so many barriers, such a huge gulf dividing your lifestyles, that you can't even envision how to make a future together work?"

The question so perfectly crystallized Jennifer's concerns about her relationship with Axel that she couldn't begin to think of a reply. She couldn't picture herself in Ax's world, either. The glitz of fame and fortune, big houses and big car collections, were at odds with her lifestyle.

Finally, the coffeemaker beeped, reminding her she needed to get back to work on the final edit of the documentary footage before showtime tonight.

"I honestly don't know the answer to that one," Jennifer answered out loud before she realized Chelsea had already vanished on those silent feet of hers, leaving an empty mug behind.

12

AXEL'S GUT KNOTTED AS the opening credits rolled on the documentary series *Double Overtime*. He hadn't wanted any part of television fame and still didn't, but with Jennifer directing and his whole team gathered at Kyle's home to watch the first installment, Ax couldn't very well ignore it.

"I'm nervous," Jennifer whispered from the leather reclining chair beside him in Kyle's posh media room.

They'd chosen seats in the back even though none of the crew would be filming the event for next week's edition of the series. So there were no lenses to hide from for once. Still, Axel would rather have her in his lap than seated beside him with the arms of both chairs separating them.

Now even Kyle's girlfriend stopped refilling drinks and passing popcorn bowls to take her place beside her man in the front row. Axel had to admit the matchmaker was a good influence on his brother, keeping hockey-crazy Kyle with one foot in the real world.

"Don't be nervous," Axel whispered back to Jennifer, lingering by her ear to breathe in the scent of her hair. "You worked really hard on this. It's going to be good."

Around them, the room went quiet as footage of their last home game filled the screen, the microphones capturing the curses and shouting on the ice better than regular game coverage would. Close-ups of the players interspersed with narration that must have been done by someone in New York since Axel didn't recognize the voice.

"Vinny!" the team shouted when the player appeared on-screen in his suburban home, talking about what it was like to play for famed Phantoms coach Nico Cesare.

"Where's Chelsea?" someone asked in the front, a question that was quickly shushed and locked down by the other guys, making Axel wonder what had happened to stop their favorite groupie from attending.

"I thought she had a role in this," Axel spoke into Jennifer's ear, glad for a chance to be close to her again.

"She does." Jennifer nodded. "Maybe she'll arrive later."

Axel was the next up on-screen as the program cut away to a practice room with him making shot after shot into a small net.

"Ax!" the players shouted. Kyle threw some popcorn at the image.

"Good transition," Axel told Jennifer, liking the way she'd gone from Vinny discussing how hard the team worked to the shot of Axel silently firing pucks into a net.

"Thank you." She took his hand in the darkness, even though bigmouthed Leandre Archambault sat on the other side of her where he could have seen the gesture.

Damn, but he liked that. He admired her grit and her fire. But Jennifer had a soft side, too, a tenderness that made her a loyal protector. A champion of the underdog. It was obvious in her film topics and evident in the care she took when she showed people on-screen. She revealed something about each person's character in the documentary.

Did she see him the way he looked in this segment, a robot worker so zeroed in on his game he didn't look up?

His cell phone vibrated in his pocket while the program switched to an interview with Coach Cesare and his wife, Lainie.

Discreetly, Axel took out his phone and clicked open the main screen to see he had a text.

Looks like U can still fire a shot. We'll expect U @ target practice tonight. Leave your brother's house alone. Someone will meet you.

"What is it?" Jennifer glanced his way, perhaps feeling the tension in him where their hands joined.

Crap.

Sweat broke out on his forehead just looking at her sitting next to him. So vulnerable because of shit he'd done in the past. He turned his ringer off and rolled his shoulders to alleviate the tension. Obviously, the Destroyers were coming for him tonight. Were probably already in position around Kyle's house. Watching.

He'd have to figure out a way to make sure Jen was somewhere safe while he took care of business.

"Nothing." He shook his head and tried to stretch his mouth into an easy grin. "Some other players ribbing me about the show."

Jen nodded, but he could see the doubt in her eyes. Her attention returned to the screen where the series showed a long shot of Vinny and Chelsea having a conversation in the parking lot behind the practice rink, their body language advertising interest in each other even if there was no sound for the image.

Interesting. Vinny damn well better take good care of Chels. Axel had identified with the loner look in her eyes the first time they'd met. He'd seen the same wariness in other gang members. The guys in motorcycle clubs were hard-asses, but most of them had gotten that way because they'd been through hell in some other part of their lives. Axel didn't know exactly what had put Chelsea on the streets as a teen, but he'd bet it had been a tough road for her.

"Chelsea should be watching with us," he observed out loud, just to make his opinion known.

"She's volunteering at a shelter tonight," Vinny Girard supplied from the other side of the room.

Some other guys shushed them as the scene swapped to the groupies in the car riding up to the Montreal game, the girls all talking about what it meant to be hockey fans.

"It's like having a family," Chelsea said on-screen, never taking her eyes from the road as she cruised up the highway toward the Canadian border.

"Yeah. A family full of kick-ass brothers," Misty piped up from the backseat, making the girls laugh in the clip. Some of the team pumped their fists in agreement around Kyle's media room.

Family. Axel turned that idea over in his head while he kept his eyes on the flat screen. Misty talked about the hard-luck backgrounds the girls had come from and the dream they shared about opening a more full-service shelter in Philadelphia that catered to women and children.

But Axel was stuck on the family idea, knowing deep in his gut that he'd been looking for that when he'd joined the Destroyers way too young. That ratty stepfather who drank like a fish and took off after a few years had paid far more attention to him than his mother ever had. So as a kid, Ax was only too happy to follow the guy into a gutted shell of a building to hang out with a bunch of seedy "uncles." Looking back, Ax understood that as a kid he'd just wanted a place to fit in. People to look out for him.

By the time he'd met Kyle Murphy, he'd been ready for a better family. A new life. But apparently he'd pissed off the old clan too much. And like any family quarrel, it had only festered over time. Tonight, he needed to end it for good.

"Get ready," Jennifer whispered to him, calling his

thoughts to the documentary series as it came back from a commercial break. "We're up next."

Trying to focus on the screen, Axel watched as game footage of him scoring a winning goal dissolved into a scene with him and Jennifer kissing in the conference room.

Massively kissing.

The media room erupted in wolf howls and shouts as a team full of grown men were transformed into twelve-year-olds at the sight of a lip-lock. Thankfully, the shot was short-lived and returned to an interview with their goalie talking about the way different guys tried to let off steam during the run for the playoffs.

"Was that what we were doing?" he asked Jennifer. "Letting off steam?" He'd sure as hell looked like a man who had it bad for Jen in that kissing shot.

How obvious would it be to his former gang that this woman was important to him?

"I lobbied for them to edit it out right up until the bitter end," she confided, leaning so close her hair slid onto his shoulder. "I even caved on the film I want to make and said I didn't care about that anymore, since you were right that my sister doesn't want any part of it. But the producer was adamant the footage would stay in since I'd already signed the waiver."

She'd been prepared to give up the film that she wanted to make so bad, no matter what her sister said. It touched him that she'd listened to his advice and consulted her sister about the project. It touched him even more that she'd gone to bat for him with her boss. That,

more than anything, told him he needed to distance himself from Jennifer while he still had a prayer of pulling
away. She was too passionately committed to the things
she cared about, too apt to want to help him fight his
battles. And he could not risk getting her involved in
whatever happened with the Destroyers.

Even if that meant he had to hurt them both in the
process. Hearts at least stood a chance of healing. But
if they came after Jennifer? His chest felt as though an
icy hand had reached inside him and squeezed.

"Nice guy you work for," he muttered darkly. "But I
need you to have some extra protection until this thing
settles out with my old gang. They'll know now that they
could get to me through you."

"What do you mean, 'settles out'? Are you going to
the police about the way that goon nearly made us get
into an accident before we left for Montreal? Because I
think that constitutes a threat." She turned toward him
in her seat, ignoring the show she'd worked so hard on
to talk to him quietly in the dark media room. "I'm your
witness. I saw it all."

Damn. Already she was searching for solutions to his
problem, eager to get involved. He couldn't have that.
The time had come to protect her even if it killed him.

Around them, the team cheered over a great stop by
the goalie during the game against Montreal. They'd all
seen it on game film, but the documentary series hyped
up the play.

"Not exactly." Axel peered around the room and saw

a clear path to the door in the back. "Would you mind missing the last half of this so we could talk about it?"

His eyes roamed over her, memorizing her beautiful features now when she looked at him with so much warmth in her gaze. He didn't want to hurt her, but it was his own damn fault for letting someone too close.

"Believe me, after all that editing, I know how it ends." Releasing his hand, she rose and headed for the back of the room.

He followed her out, leaving his empty popcorn container on a table by the exit. He levered open the door, careful not to let too much light into the viewing room.

The sound from the documentary was still audible here, and Axel gestured for her to follow him toward a game room near the indoor hot tub. The scent of chlorine hung in the air as they passed an indoor pool and reached an oversize den with a billiard table and dartboard. A bar and a foosball game filled out the room while trophies and framed jerseys covered the walls.

"Wow." Jennifer craned her neck to see all the game photos and magazine covers on the wall. "Kyle has quite a spread, doesn't he?"

"You mean the trophies?" His gaze went to the floor-to-ceiling cases of awards his foster brother had snagged over the years. He was just as glad to delay their conversation since that meant he'd have a few more minutes with her.

A little time to soak in everything he'd grown to admire. Damn it, his legs felt like lead with this weight hanging over him.

"I mean the house." Jennifer ran her hand over the Lucite bar lit from underneath. "I've never seen anything like it."

"It's nice," he agreed. "It belonged to a former football player, so it already had a lot of the extras, and Kyle has been adding bonus features since the moment we touched down in Philly. But about tonight—"

"Professional athletes have some seriously nice digs." She moved toward the silver saddle chairs that looked like something out of a '50s diner. "Sorry to gawk, but I've never hung out with hockey stars on my jobs before. I'm usually camping in some overheated trailer and feeling guilty about all my luxuries as I film the lives of—"

"Jen, this is important." He redirected her, on edge about the meeting tonight. Could there be a worse time for this discussion? Dragging out one of the bar stools, he motioned toward it. "Have a seat."

She bristled but did as he asked. Her red waves flounced as she dropped into the chair, her yellow skirt printed with limes and mangoes fanning out around her.

"So why don't you want to go to the police about the threat?" she asked, crossing slender legs so that a green suede ankle boot brushed his calf.

"It wouldn't be enough of a threat for the authorities to take seriously." Pointing a finger at them like a gun and pulling an imaginary trigger? That'd get him laughed out of the local precinct.

"How do you know that until you file a formal complaint?"

"I was on the sketchy side of the law long enough to know how it works."

"But that was in a foreign country. You're on U.S. soil now." Uncrossing her legs, she leaned forward to emphasize her point, her white T-shirt with an iconic film-reel design stretching across her breasts.

Damn but he wished he could think about that right now instead of being scared for her safety. The sooner he put some distance between them, the better. He'd been an idiot not to send her running back to New York the first day she'd shown up at the practice rink, but he'd gotten sucked in by her impulsive charm and undeniable sex appeal.

"Right. I'm in the U.S. now, where I could be deported if I'm not careful."

"You haven't done anything wrong." She pounded a fist on the bar, clearly indignant at the thought of injustice.

In that moment, he could picture her making the documentaries she enjoyed most, her zeal for her work driving the project forward. It would be nice to be worthy of a woman like that. To be a man who didn't have a lousy past tied around his neck like an albatross.

"I know you think I should go to the cops. But first, I'm going to speak to the local branch of the Destroyers and see what they want." His cell phone burned a hole in his pocket, the text message assuring him there would be someone watching for him to leave Kyle's tonight. Someone keeping tabs on him.

And that meant they would likely be on the lookout

for Jennifer, too. His hands fisted and his determination solidified.

Jennifer reeled from Axel's announcement, trying to figure out if she could have possibly misunderstood him.

"Are you insane?" She gripped his shoulders and faced him head-on. "You can't do that."

She'd researched the Destroyers after Axel had told her about his past and they were bad eggs. Notorious for drug running and brawling with rival gangs, they were trouble on both sides of the ocean.

"I have to." He didn't look swayed in the least.

"No." She shook her head, refusing to hear it. "Ax, it's dangerous. There are other—"

"Don't you think I know it's dangerous?" He stood, walking away from her when she needed to hang on to him with both hands. "I rode with them for years. I know exactly how they'll handle this situation."

Her stomach knotted tighter while he absently rolled the eight ball around the empty billiard table.

"You do?"

"Yes." When the ball sank in a far pocket, he reached beneath the table and pulled out two others to spin across the felt. "They're watching the house. They'll surround my car on the way home, insist I ride with them to their stronghold. Then, after a few bullshit moves meant to intimidate me, they'll blackmail me with my past and name their terms for their silence. If I don't give them what they want, they'll go after you next."

"Me?" she squeaked before she cleared her throat. "Isn't that all the more reason to involve the authorities?"

"No. That's the best incentive to keep this quiet. If I rat them out, the consequences go from dangerous to deadly." The certainty in his voice terrified her.

Suddenly, she didn't care about their differences. About how a future between them didn't add up. She just wanted him safe. Whole.

Most of all, she wanted him to stay here for the night where they wouldn't come after him.

"Then let's wait until morning to figure out what to do. We'll ask your brother for help. Your family has connections. You can spend the night here—"

"I can't." He pulled out his cell phone. Maybe he checked the time or a message, because he only glanced at it before he returned it to his pants pocket. "I don't want them gunning for my family any more than I want them to come after you, so Kyle can't know any more about this than he already does."

"Of course, but—"

"Jen. This isn't going to work." He stalked toward her, leaving the billiard table behind.

"That's what I've been saying." She reached for him, her fingers landing on the immovable wall of his chest. "Your plan is too dangerous."

"No. I mean you and I." His blue eyes were icy. Resolute. "We've known all along this was going to be difficult and having that kiss aired on television increased the problem one-hundred-fold."

He couldn't be serious.

"Axel, don't push me away just because of this." Needing to impress her point upon him, she shackled one thick forearm with both her hands. "We can figure this out."

"It's not just because of this. Even if we take the Destroyers out of the equation, there's still a huge disconnect between you living and working in New York and me based in Philadelphia and traveling the country." He swallowed hard and for a second she thought he was going to pull her into his arms and kiss her. Tell her that he was dead wrong and she was right and that they needed to go to the police.

But then, there was silence.

"We haven't even discussed that yet, so why borrow trouble?" Her fingers squeezed tighter even though she knew that holding him there was the worst kind of clingy. "Let's figure this out first, then we can worry about what will happen when I go back to New York."

Clingy or not, she realized she'd never had a man worth hanging on to until now.

"Jen, maybe if this stuff with my past hadn't come along, I would have been content to coast through the next few weeks and just enjoy what we have. But you can't tell me that—even without the Destroyers—we would have made this work long-term." He spoke like a reasonable stranger, his expression so cool and remote. His accent thicker than usual. "You are a social crusader with a mission for justice and equality. You thrive on championing the underdog. How will you feel in my world where all the houses look like this?"

He made a sweeping gesture around Kyle's extravagant game room. The scent of the indoor pool still clung in her nose.

"Those things are just superficial," she argued, even though she'd been a little worried about that herself.

And why did he have to bring it up now, before they'd even gotten time to work through those problems?

"Right. And you'll always see them as superficial, even when I buy another new car instead of donating to a charity." He had hit her in a vulnerable spot, since the cars did strike her as over-the-top. "I saw the judgment in your eyes when you looked at the vehicles in my garage last night."

"Stop." She felt panicky, as if she'd been pushed backward and there was no one to stop her endless fall. "I know you're just doing this because of the danger I could be in, and that's not going to go away even if we break up right now."

Right? That had to be why he was doing this now. She swallowed hard, waiting for him to say that he didn't mean it.

Carefully, he pried her fingers from his arm and collected her hands in his.

"I'm sorry, Jennifer." He kissed the back of one hand, his distant, polite manner bearing no resemblance to the charming cretin who'd stomped into her life on skates after a sweaty practice earlier that week.

"Damn you, Axel." She wrenched her hands away from him, hurt to the core even though she shouldn't be. Even though there was no way a woman could care so much for a man she'd only just met.

And oh, God, who was she kidding? Not once in her life had she slept with a man she didn't *l-o-v-e*. Would spelling it make it any less real, she wondered? Any less true?

"Jennifer, I have to leave." He stuffed his hands in his pockets. "I already talked Kyle and Marissa into giving your camera guys an at-home interview tonight, which will keep Kyle too occupied to follow me. Marissa has offered for you to stay overnight afterward so I know you're safe."

"Do you honestly think you can dictate where I spend the night or orchestrate my life for me when you're willing to walk away over this?" Sure, she hadn't wanted to be a trophy girlfriend of some wealthy NHL player. But Ax was more than that.

They could figure out something if they stayed together. Fought for a future.

"I'm trusting you not to put your life in danger for a relationship that was never going to work anyhow. But if I have to, I'll call Kyle and he'll make sure you stay put for the night."

Anger and hurt fired through her, but he was so cool and distant she knew he'd made up his mind. No amount of arguing was going to change it.

"You're making a mistake," she told him finally, hearing the media room doors open in the hallway and the sounds of the team filtering out into the corridor.

"I'm fixing a mistake," he told her, his square jaw flexing. "I should have done it a long time ago."

13

"ARE YOU MAD AT ME?"

Misty's question was the first thing Chelsea heard when she answered her cell phone shortly after midnight.

Exhausted from her last-minute volunteer shift at the shelter and even more drained from her encounter with Vinny the night before, Chelsea sank onto the futon in her tiny living room. She pulled the homemade afghan, a gift from a long-ago social worker, onto her lap.

"Hmm. That begs the question, do I have a reason to be mad at you?" Tipping her head against the futon cushion, she closed her eyes for a moment until she remembered that Misty was still in New York with her SUV. She bolted upright in her seat. "Oh, God. You didn't get in an accident, did you? Are you okay?"

"I'm fine. The car is fine." Misty's singsong voice assured her. "You didn't watch the first installment of the Phantoms documentary series, did you?"

"Not yet." Grabbing the remote, she flipped on her

television and the ancient VCR player beneath it. She was happy with her tag-sale furnishings and Craigslist purchases for the most part, but one of these days she needed to update her electronics. "Although, using my ever-reliable technology from a million years ago, I did try to record it."

She rewound the tape long enough to see footage of the game in New York. Still, she didn't have the heart to watch the show tonight. In the end, she'd given the director permission to use the clips of her and Vinny. When she'd said yes, she'd been excited about the possibility of seeing him more. Of moving toward some kind of real relationship with a guy she already trusted.

That was before she'd been scared spitless at the thought of meeting his parents.

"Oh." Misty paused awkwardly, an uncommon occurrence for the woman who had an answer to everything. "Well, then. I might as well prepare you."

"For what?" Her imagination ran wild. What if Vinny denounced her on national TV? Or what if someone researched her past and revealed private things about her that she wouldn't want other people to know? That she'd been kicked out of that one gym, for example, where she'd used a fake membership card....

"Nothing big," Misty rushed to reassure her, although that was too little too late. "I just...I didn't realize they were going to show the footage where I talked about your dream of running a shelter geared toward women and children."

"You broadcast my dreams on television?" Chelsea's

finger hit the rewind button again—she needed to find out the extent of the damage.

Was privacy so much to ask for? Yes, safety and security came first. Yet after all the homeless years, after all the nights in shelters where anyone could walk past your bed while you were sleeping…damn it, she treasured her privacy.

"I didn't think it was secret, per se—"

"But you knew I wouldn't be happy about it or you wouldn't have called asking if I'm mad at you." She came to the start and hit Play. "Damn it, Misty, you of all people know—"

"Look, Chels. Never mind. I'm not sorry and I did it on purpose, okay?" She blurted the words. "Maybe that's half the reason I wanted to visit family, just in case you were going to freak out on me. But I'm your friend, and I love you. You deserve to have that shelter and I wanted to put it out there in the public eye where—"

"What are you thinking?" Chelsea hit Fast-forward, but stopped dead when the screen came to her and Vinny talking. Oh, God. Her chest felt as if it had caved in, and she forgot to be mad at her best friend.

"I'm thinking that it doesn't hurt to share a dream on the most popular cable network in the world," Misty countered. "You're a sweet girl with a big heart and one of the sharpest, most streetwise people I know. Viewers are going to see that. And by morning, some rich philanthropist is going to want to donate a jillion dollars to make sure you have the chance to do good in the world…. Chels?" Misty cut the diatribe suddenly short.

Chelsea tried to breathe past the lump in her throat and the pain in her chest.

"Yeah?" She clutched her afghan, thumbs winding through the purple-and-blue yarn. Not even the feel of her favorite things—the sight of her spotlessly clean little apartment—could ease the ache in her chest.

"I thought you'd cut me off or yell at me." Misty sounded thoughtful. "Are you, like, genuinely furious?"

"No." Her VCR was paused on the image of her and Vinny. The guy whose number was the first one she'd ever tattooed on her body. "I broke things off between me and Vinny, and I'm such an idiot."

"You are not an idiot." Misty took on her battle-general voice and it made Chelsea smile that she could envision her friend's pursed lips and drawn-in cheeks perfectly. They'd lifted each other up through a lot of hard times.

But she couldn't imagine feeling uplifted now, when she'd run scared from the best—the nicest—thing to ever happen to her.

"He wanted to introduce me to his parents." She trembled inside just thinking about it. And she knew it was stupid that she was smart enough to survive homelessness and tough enough to outfox a coked-up teenager intent on raping her, yet the thought of meeting a couple of nice, ordinary Midwesterners frightened her to death.

But there it was.

"Well, of course you're scared." Misty said it as if it was the most reasonable thing in the world.

She loved Misty. Loved. Her.

"Really?"

"Perfectly normal girls who are brought up in brownstones and go to private schools are scared to meet their boyfriends' parents."

"He's not exactly my boyfriend." Her gaze went to the Phantoms poster on the wall above the TV, her eyes easily finding Vinny's face amid all his teammates.

"He wants to be," Misty told her. The sounds of the city emanated in the background. Horns honking. Brakes squealing. "He just put the cart ahead of the horse because he's excited to finally spend time with you. You're so great that of course he wants his parents to meet you and see how awesome you are."

"Right." Chelsea wrapped the afghan around herself and shuffled into the kitchen so she could forage in the cabinets for something to eat. "I can hear it now, 'Mom, Dad, meet Chelsea, professional groupie and former resident of the streets.' I'm sure his parents will be impressed."

"I won't dignify that with a response. You know I'm right. And didn't we agree that when we are running our own shelter there will be positive affirmations? Opportunities for people with battered self-esteem to grow?" Misty rattled off phrases that Chelsea herself had used more than once when talking about the kind of shelter she wanted to run one day.

"This is different." Her hand went to the place on her chest where Vinny's number rested. Her heart ached right there.

"It's not different. Be the change you want to see in

the world, right? We've got to forge the path to normal so that other women can see it's possible. You need to believe in yourself, Chelsea." Misty's subtle croon had talked hundreds of rich women into buying expensive makeup packages back in those days of her first job at a cosmetics counter. She could be very persuasive. "How can we spout our ideals to others unless we've taken the risks to back them up ourselves?"

Chelsea turned back toward the living room, her VCR still paused on the image of her and Vinny. His warm hazel eyes and easy smile called to her. She could imagine his voice tinged with good humor as he told her about rounding up the stray cow the night before a big game. Most of all, she remembered his indignant anger at the night she'd been so scared in that pool house all alone.

He was a great guy. Maybe he deserved better.

But if he really wanted her... She was going to gather her courage and ask him for another chance.

IT DIDN'T MATTER WHERE Axel drove. He knew his past would find him. And on cue, five miles outside of Philly's Chestnut Hill neighborhood, the sound of Harley engines rumbled in his ears.

He wasn't surprised when the distinctive single headlights filled his rearview, a swarm of Hogs bearing down on him. Someone must have followed him more discreetly out of Kyle's neighborhood, then alerted the rest to fall in line.

Axel told himself it was a good thing he'd parted

ways with Jennifer. He didn't want her mixed up in this and he wouldn't let her be targeted because of him. He liked the idea of her safe at Kyle's house for the night, even if she was angry.

Hurt.

Pulling the Escalade off the road, Axel felt the answering twinge in his chest far more than he felt any kind of fear for himself tonight. If anything, he was spoiling for a fight since threats from these bastards had cost him Jennifer.

He pushed the button to roll down his power window, knowing there would be a representative goon out there. Axel understood the job of the enforcer all too well. It was a role he'd taken on with every team he'd ever played for. The rough-looking dude with a beard down to his chest and wraparound shades over his eyes—How the hell could he see anything in the dark?—wasn't all that different from him.

"Follow us," the big guy grunted, leather vest creaking as he straightened. "And don't even think about trying to ditch us or we'll go back for the redhead."

"I want to meet with the brains behind this dumb-ass operation, you prick," Axel shouted out the window at the guy's retreating back. "If you threaten her again, things are going to turn ugly in a hurry."

Not because he could really back up that statement. More because he'd likely pull a berserker and take out as many of the motorcycle dudes as possible before someone popped him.

Thankfully, the beast in leather kept walking to his

bike while the rest of the crew—maybe ten of them—kept vigil from the comfort of their Harleys. No one said anything, apparently unimpressed with Ax's threat.

Fifteen minutes later, down back roads and through some run-down suburbs, the motorcycle brigade led him to a dark warehouse with boards on the windows. Wide overhead bays were built high on one wall, probably designed for loading tractor trailers. As they approached, a normal-size door opened on the side of the low cement building, light spilling out into the surrounding woods.

Ax stepped out of the Escalade before they could come for him, ready to get this over with. His nerves twitched now as his biker escorts surrounded him, ensuring he didn't run. As if he would. With Jen at risk, he was very ready to negotiate with these guys.

Nearing the entrance, he heard the guitar riffs from an old Southern rock song and laughter from inside the building. The abandoned facility must be a flophouse for the gang rather than a place designated for violence. Good news, that.

"Welcome back, Akseli." The Finnish words floated on the spring breeze, the language so fluid and natural to his ear that it took him a minute to recall how out of place it was.

A familiar figure stood in the shadowy archway, shocking the hell out of him. Tall and bow-legged, a cigarette perched on a fat lower lip. A generous gut spilled over his belt, his leather vest too small to ever button again. Jaako Latt, the boss of the gang back in Helsinki, waited for him.

"Didn't trust the locals to do your dirty work, Jaako?" Axel steeled himself the same way he did before a fight on the ice. He tightened his abs. Kept his shoulders low. His fists ready to fly at the slightest provocation.

He didn't realize he'd stopped short until one of the bikers nudged his shoulder, prodding him forward.

"No," Jaako said in Finnish. Then swapping to English, he barked at the horde of Destroyers accompanying Axel. The guy was probably only in his late fifties, but he'd aged well beyond his years. Scars riddled his face and his voice was rough from a two-pack-per-day habit. "No. We don't need to push one of our own. Come in, Akseli. I've traveled a long way to collect on your debt."

"Ever heard of email?" Axel stepped into the clubhouse decked out like a crappy tavern with no health code to worry about.

A bar made of an old countertop stood against one wall with cases of liquor stacked nearby. Dusty plastic cups and a dorm-size fridge rounded out the self-serve operation. A few sawhorse tables were filled with bottles of beer and cards, as if they'd walked in on a game of poker. Ax didn't see any weapons, but he'd bet money most of the guys—even a couple of women—packed heat.

"The internet is not secure for our business, I do not think," the old-timer said, his gait stiff on one side as he shuffled toward the bar. Bullet wound, Axel guessed. "I am retiring and have come to collect. You are my retirement, you see. I let you go. Now, you finance my way out. Though, of course, I leave with honor. Unlike you."

"You want money?" Axel spoke in English.

Jaako stuck to Finnish when he replied. "You will pay to keep the crimes of your past a secret from your American fans and the woman you kiss on television. This way, you protect your endorsement deals, yes?" Jaako took a long drag on the butt in his mouth before tossing it on the dusty cement floor. "One time payment. Cash. Say, three million?"

The Southern rock music kept on playing, the volume cranked even though Axel guessed half the guys in the room kept careful tabs on the conversation.

Shit. Jaako had a point about protecting his image since endorsement deals didn't go to players with skeletons in their closets. But protecting Jen was a whole hell of a lot more important than preserving an image. He was furious over having to hurt Jennifer because of his past.

He opened his mouth. Fully prepared to tell them to go to hell and see what happened.

"I don't think so, dirtbag," a familiar female voice shouted.

Axel's stomach dropped. Blood froze. Fear crawled up his spine.

Every head in the room swiveled to see the source of that declaration. Jennifer stood in the doorway, her slender arm squeezed in the rough hold of a half-wit teenage biker who gripped her in one hand and a video camera in the other.

"Quiet," snarled the gangster who held her. "I found her in a tree, holding the camera up to that window," the kid told Jaako, pointing to the boarded-up glass in question.

She must have found a crack in the boards to film through.

"Let her go." Axel moved toward her, but five guys rose out of their chairs to stop him. Ten hands had to hold him back.

"Break the camera," Jaako told the kid in his thickly accented English. "You have done well. She is good persuasion for our hockey star."

"I'm only persuaded if you let her go right this second." Axel never took his eyes off the kid with a death wish who still gripped Jennifer's arm so hard there were going to be bruises.

At a nod from Jaako, the teenage gangster-in-training released her. Ax's relief was short-lived since she didn't fade quietly into the background while he talked them out of here.

She stepped closer to the Finnish boss.

"Break the camera all you want," she taunted him. "The feed goes directly to a URL that records all the footage." Her green eyes flashed with the kind of daring most men wouldn't have facing down this crowd.

But then, not many people were born with a fire inside. And as much as he admired that about her, he really needed her to quit egging on the man who could wreak vengeance with a nod to his underlings.

"Don't you get it?" she pressed, her yellow skirt with

the mangoes and limes absurdly out of place among the leather- and denim-clad bikers. With guns.

"Get what, Red?" Jaako barked at her. "You are a foolish woman who wanders where you do not belong."

"I have evidence of blackmail. You'll go to jail for that. At the very least, you're getting booted out of the U.S. and you won't ever be allowed back in."

Jaako cackled, a new cigarette nearly falling out of his mouth. "As if we were strangers to criminal charges. Even if I cared about your blackmail claim, I know you won't use the film to free Akseli of his obligation to me because he does not want his fans to discover his criminal past. Your threat is useless."

JENNIFER FELT HERSELF DEFLATE.

She hadn't thought about that. Axel would be implicated if she exposed his blackmailing former gang for the scumbags they were. She'd followed Axel out here, leaving two seconds behind him to avoid detection by Kyle Murphy.

Because whether or not Axel wanted to be with her, she didn't want him hurt. Or threatened. She loved him.

She'd called the cops when she'd seen the motorcycles pull him over, but since she was from out of town, she hadn't been able to say exactly where they were. Then, when the police dispatcher had told her to stay in her car once she'd reached the warehouse, she'd ignored him, thinking she could help Axel somehow.

Yet she'd only made herself a liability in this show-down. Her eyes went to Axel. She met his blue gaze, hoping he knew how sorry she was for intervening. For acting impulsively and thinking she could fix everything once again.

"You're brilliant," Axel told her, the U-shaped scar on his face stretching as he gave her a grim smile. "Because I'm going public with my past. Kyle knows all about it anyhow, so if I don't come back tonight, he'll go to the media for me. Either way, I plan to share the trouble I got in as a kid in order to help other kids stay out of danger."

"Really?" Jennifer knew his career would take a hit. That the announcement would be a distraction during the playoffs when the whole team needed to focus.

"Don't be stupid," the old Finnish biker yelled at him. "Three million is nothing to pay. You owe the Destroyers for taking you in. You swore allegiance then turned your back on us when a better offer came along."

Jennifer edged closer to Axel, even though a handful of guys still surrounded him. Restrained him from coming toward her.

"You can't blackmail someone who freely admits what they've done," Axel clarified. "But you can damn well be busted for trying, thanks to the live video feed. Good thing a prominent New York producer got it all on film."

Curses flew in Finnish. The cigarette fell out of the ringleader's mouth. Even the local bikers looked surprised. Confused at the outburst since they didn't seem to understand Finnish any better than she did.

But every last one of them understood police sirens.

And the long, high wail sounded close outside the building.

"Jen." Axel grabbed her while the bikers who had held him scrambled for the exit. "Come here."

He pulled her around the towering cases of alcohol, then drew her down to crouch behind the bar.

"We're the good guys, Axel," she reminded him, her shoes sticking in spilled beer. "We don't need to hi—"

Gunfire broke out before the sentence had fully left her mouth.

She would have screamed, but Axel crushed her to his chest, holding her tight. Putting his body between her and the bar, providing an extra barrier for the bullets. Fear spiked. The acrid sent of gun smoke wafted on the air.

"It's okay. It's outside," he assured her, the shots replaced by more shouting and sirens. The sound of motorcycle engines firing. "You called the cops?"

She breathed in the scent of his skin, her fingers clutching at his muscles straining the fabric of his cotton button-down. She focused on him instead of the chaos and fear. He was so familiar. So strong and capable.

Nodding, she swallowed back the panic, her spine pinned against liquor boxes and a fallen bar stool.

"I had to. After I followed you, I saw all those motorcycles surround you. I knew you'd be mad that I got the police involved, but I couldn't just let those guys take you. I was so scared."

He hugged her again, his powerful arms making her feel safe in spite of the scuffle outside.

"You? Scared?" he asked, pulling back to cup her face in his big, roughened hands. "I would have never guessed."

"Don't be ridiculous," she chided, hoping he was hugging her because he wanted to hug her and not just because he was glad she was okay. "Who wouldn't be scared to face down a biker gang? And that snot-nosed teenager frightened me so bad I almost fell out of the tree."

She showed him the scratch on her arm where a branch had nicked her. Her heart beat erratically and she wondered if she could be in shock. Did people go into shock from seeing their loved ones threatened?

"I told you to stay at Kyle's," he told her, his voice turning harsh and ragged. "Damn it, why didn't you listen? You could have been killed."

"Don't you yell at me, Axel Rankin." She willed her heart to slow down. Her breath to ease up before she started hyperventilating. "I've had about all I can take for one night."

She scowled at him until he stopped scowling at her. All she really cared about was finding out whether or not he wanted to be with her. Had he walked away from her because he wanted to scare her off tonight? Or did he truly feel that it could never work out between them?

Just as she was going to demand an answer, there was a loud bang nearby and a shout over a bullhorn.

"Police! Come out with your hands up!"

14

THANK GOD THE SENIOR ranking officer on the job was a Phantoms fan.

Axel sat in a downtown police precinct an hour later, grateful he and Jennifer hadn't been arrested. They'd been brought in for questioning about the events of the evening, however, and been separated so the police could compare their stories. Axel hadn't seen Jennifer since they'd been patted down by the police who'd entered the warehouse. The officers had found an impressive weapons stash, ensuring the Destroyers would be brought up on charges. Jaako Latt had been implicated by all the local bikers, the gang's oath of loyalty not standing up so well for the Finnish ringleader. Apparently some of the Philly members hadn't been too pleased that they'd risked their necks for a foreigner who planned to blackmail a former member and keep the profits to himself.

Or so Ax had heard from his new police friends. He just wished he'd get an update on Jennifer now that it seemed as though he could put his past to rest.

"You know you've got to call Dad," Kyle told Axel for the second time since he'd shown up at the station. Axel had phoned Kyle as soon as they were brought in, and although Kyle was furious that Axel had met with the Destroyers without him, he'd shown up in record time to help him out.

They sat in front of the desk where Axel had given his statement, and up until a few minutes ago, a crowd of officers had circled around them, each with input on how the Phantoms should play their first opponent in the playoffs, the Boston Bears. The crowd had dissipated after a call came in with a lead on where some of the other bikers had taken refuge after the bust at the warehouse. Phones rang almost continuously in the understaffed precinct, and the scent of coffee and take-out food hung in the air. Kyle's phone beeped with a new text message every five minutes.

"And tell him what? I nearly got arrested? Almost got someone I care about killed?" Axel leaned back in the creaky wooden chair, wishing Jennifer would walk out of one of the other rooms. He needed to see her. Reassure himself she was okay. He'd have nightmares about her showing up at that clubhouse for a long time. "Or did you want me to warn Dad that I may get booted out of the league for being a crap role model to kids everywhere?"

"Look. Ax." Kyle kicked the bottom of Axel's chair with one foot, forcing the legs down to the ground. "I've got to tell you something."

"I know there was nothing you could do about Jennifer sneaking out of your house." He didn't want Kyle to feel bad about how things shook down. "She must have left seconds after me, so you were probably still down in the media room."

"I feel terrible about that, man. But there's something else." He stroked a hand across his chin, a gesture Axel recognized from way back. A guilty tell.

"What?"

"When you called me tonight, I called Dad."

"Damn it, Kyle, you had no right—"

"I know, but I'm not sorry. He's a smart guy and he knows stuff we don't, okay?" Kyle pulled some paperwork out of his back pocket. Unfolding the sheaf, he smoothed out the crinkles. "Dad said we should hire a publicist. Someone to be ready if you needed help spinning this whole thing."

"I don't want to *spin* anything." Axel had been ducking his past for too long, hoping it wouldn't come back to bite him in the ass. And it might have cost him Jennifer forever. "I'm going with the straight-up truth."

"Okay, maybe *spin* isn't the right word." Kyle passed him the papers. "But you need someone to help tell your side of the story so people understand you the way we do. If you could fill in some of the blanks here, we could fire off a press release tonight."

Axel shook his head, although on first glance, the list of ideas for a press release opening were all kind of good. None of them made him sound pathetic or as if he was asking for sympathy. Damn. His foster father only hired the best. This publicist must be good.

"Too bad the news deadlines must have passed already." He shoved aside the release. "It's late. But maybe I could talk to this PR person tomorrow and see if we could do something."

"Actually, the NBA playoffs started tonight, with a series on the West Coast that went into overtime." Kyle flashed his iPhone in front of Axel, showing him the score. "So the sports page is still being finalized, according to the publicist. We could run something now, but you need to put a call in to this guy."

Axel stared at Kyle's phone as his brother pushed it toward him. He hadn't wanted help dealing with his past. Had avoided dragging the Murphys into this mess for years. But his foster family had proven once again that they were there for him.

"Thanks, bro." Axel had to clear his throat, the words sounding rough from too many emotions.

Kyle bumped his fist. "I'm still mad I didn't get to go kick Jaako's ass. But if this helps you put the whole thing to rest, that's cool."

"I owe you one." He pressed the call button on the contact Kyle had highlighted on the phone. "Now I just have to figure out how to get my girl back."

Because this night wouldn't be truly behind him until he had Jennifer in his arms again. Until she'd forgiven him for trying to break up with her and nearly getting her killed.

It was going to be a long night.

THE PHANTOMS MADE BIG headlines in the local press.

Vincent Girard couldn't think of anyone who would

be more interested in all the news about the team than Chelsea. Or so he told himself as he stood with a folded paper under one arm, his finger hovering over the buzzer to apartment 2B. He clutched a tray from Arnie's Coffee in his hand, knowing he probably looked desperate to show up on her doorstep at…7:15 a.m., according to his watch.

Yeah, well. Go big, or go home. He hadn't waited patiently for Chelsea to come around this season only to lose her in a moment of brainlessness. The memory of her curled against him on the plane had kept him awake all night, reminding him how close he'd come to making her his. How could she have ever thought she wouldn't be good enough to meet his parents when she'd accomplished so much with so little?

He stared up at the neat brick building and jabbed the intercom button with new resolve.

The next twelve seconds felt longer than a penalty kill. Finally, the speaker on the wall of her building crackled to life.

"Hello?" Her voice sounded vaguely wary, but wide-awake. He'd seen her often enough around morning practices to know she was an early riser.

Like him.

"Chelsea." Just saying her name felt good. "It's Vinny. I know you probably don't—"

The buzzer on the security door vibrated to life, admitting him. He yanked it open before she changed her mind, shocked that she would allow him into her home before he even got out an apology. He knew how much importance she placed on privacy. Security.

Taking the steps two at a time, he kept the coffee tray level, careful not to spill any. He didn't need to look at the numbers to find 2B because a door creaked open at the end of the hallway before he reached the top of the stairs.

She stood in the archway, hair still damp from a shower. In short sleeves, she revealed the little tattoos of his teammates' numbers on her arms and he wondered if he'd see his somewhere. Her knit pajama pants were covered in blue Phantoms logos. Even better, she wore a white T-shirt with his number on it, an item sold in the gift shop where she worked. That had to be a good sign, right?

"I brought you coffee," he started, holding out his offering as he reached her braided front mat in quick strides. "The newspaper, too. There's a lot of stuff about the team and the documentary debut. Plus Axel announced—"

"Vinny, I'm so sorry I flipped out about meeting your parents." She ignored the coffee and the paper, her eyebrows furrowed with worry he wished he'd never put there.

But oh, man, this felt like a second chance to him. Relief flooded through him so fast he thought he'd better sit down soon.

"It's my fault for getting ahead of myself. I'm the one who's sorry." He peered past her into her apartment. "Do

you want to get dressed and go for a walk or something?
I didn't mean to invade your space or anything—"

Her arms were around his neck before he finished.
Soft, cinnamon-flavored lips met his, stirring a hunger
he didn't think he'd ever fill. The feel of her over-
whelmed him, bombarding his senses as her soft breasts
molded to his chest and the clean scent of her shampoo
drifted to his nose. His breath evaporated for a long
minute, and when it returned, his lungs dragged in the
air so fast he felt light-headed.

Chelsea was kissing him.

Beyond the tangible, physical evidence of his personal goddess against him, he also had the knowledge
that she still cared. That she wanted him, too, even if
she wasn't ready for all of him yet. Knowing that damn
near brought him to his knees.

"Chelsea." He levered back, breaking the kiss. "I'm
dying to hold you, sweetheart. But I need to set down
the coffee."

Her passion-dazed eyes fired him up like nothing
else. She blinked slowly, her lips swollen from their
kisses.

"Of course." She took the paper from under his arm
and drew him inside. "I didn't mean to throw myself at
you. I don't know what came over me."

He locked the door behind them, setting the coffee on
a stand near the sofa. He had the vague impression of a
homey, warm apartment that smelled like wood polish
and lemon. But mostly, he only had eyes for her, his
heartbeat pounding in his chest at being allowed inside

when he'd been worried she wouldn't even let him apologize.

"I hope it comes over you again," he confided. "Often." He had to force himself not to grab her by the waist and tug her back into his arms.

A warm light glittered in her eyes and he could imagine the way she might flirt with him one day when she was more comfortable. When he'd won her trust completely.

"I think it might." She stood in the middle of the living room near a cream-colored futon covered in a bright blanket. "I don't have much experience with men. But now that I've given myself a chance to really consider what it would be like to be with you, I've been preoccupied with…" She made a vague gesture with her hand. "The idea of us together. Um. Intimately."

He'd taken slap shots to the face that stunned him less.

"Damn." Surprise and red-hot desire joined forces to knock the breath out of him again and he lowered himself to the nearest seat, which just happened to be a coffee table. "You can't imagine what that does to me."

"In a good way, though, right?" The worried note crept into her voice. "When I say I'm inexperienced, I mean really inexperienced. As in virginal. So, you might have to spell some things out for me. Although, obviously, I know the basics."

Possessiveness tightened inside him. He was seized with the urge to pull her into the bedroom and give her an all-day education. Except he knew she wasn't ready.

The incident two nights ago had reinforced the knowledge that he had to take things slow. Careful. Because
Chelsea was going to be his forever mate. The woman
he loved. The woman he would marry one day.

She'd already given him a second chance. Not for all
the world would he spoil it.

"Everything about you pleases me," he assured her,
rising to his feet. "You don't need to worry about anything because when it happens between us, it's going to
be the best. But there's no rush because I'm willing to
wait however long it takes."

He ran his hands over her shoulders, liking the way
his jersey number looked on her slender body. He felt
her relax and the color of her eyes deepened. Somehow,
he knew the slower approach was the right decision.

"Okay." She nodded, agreeing to take things slow.
"But first I want to show you something and I hope you
don't think it's too forward of me in light of what we've
decided about waiting."

Visions of what she might display had his mouth watering. His body so hard and his skin so tight that he
could only nod. Yeah, waiting wasn't going to be a cake-
walk, but for her…he'd manage. He swallowed hard, pre-
paring himself.

"I think it's fate that we ended up dating," she said,
shuffling closer so they stood mere inches apart. "Because you were my first—" she tugged on the V-neck
of her T-shirt, sliding the fabric aside to reveal more
creamy skin just above her left breast "—tattoo."

Words escaped him. The combination of a sensual

offering and seeing his number scrawled over her heart solidified every instinct he'd had toward her from the first day they'd met.

Slowly, he lowered his head to her breast, giving her time to pull back. She didn't. Instead, she arched toward him, lifting herself closer to his lips. With his blood pounding in his ears, he kissed her there, inhaling the fragrance of her faint citrus perfume. Then, knowing she wanted more, he licked her lightly. Gently. Teased a sigh from her and a groan from him.

But no more. Not yet.

"I'm so crazy about you, Chelsea," he confided, wanting to bare his heart, too. "I always have been."

"And I'm your biggest fan," she whispered back, falling into his arms the way she had a million times in his dreams.

"I NEED TO SEE HER RIGHT now," Axel Rankin demanded outside the room where Jennifer had been questioned by the police. "She's answered more than enough questions and she's here of her own free will. I'm taking her home."

Inside the tiny room where she'd given her statement to a nice female police officer, Jennifer smiled. She could hear Axel in the hallway, demanding her release.

She hadn't seen him after they were taken in to make formal complaints against the biker gang. During the night, she'd had a powwow with a Murphy family lawyer to be sure her rights were respected throughout the process. Kyle had been in to check on her at various times, and he'd told her Axel hadn't been arrested, thank God. But with all the paperwork to sign, she realized she'd been here for so long the sun was already up. She'd been finished for nearly an hour, she'd just needed to check in with her boss. He'd left her a million messages after the good ratings news about the hockey documentary. The show had been a hit.

"Colin," she told her boss over the phone as Axel charged into the narrow room. "I'm thrilled about the ratings and I'm glad we're in good shape for next week. But I've got an important meeting that I need to take. I'll have to call you back."

She disconnected the call, knowing that Axel mattered more than her micromanaging boss.

"Morning," she chirped nervously, unsure how to read his mood. The last time they'd spoken privately, they'd been crouched behind a bar while bullets flew around them and he'd been angry with her for following him to the warehouse.

Was he still upset? More important, did he still think they ought to part ways?

"How are you?" he asked, polite but somehow too formal.

Was it her imagination or was he more distant today? He wore a clean blue button-down and khakis, his shirt open at the collar with a gray T-shirt underneath. Kyle must have brought him clothes during the night after Axel had called him.

"Fine. They're done with me, I was just checking in with work." Her eyes raked over him as she remembered how he'd planted himself between her and the flying bullets, protecting her when she'd been too shell-shocked to understand what was happening. His big, strong body had sheltered her.

Would it be the last time he touched her?

"Good. My brother left a car for us so I can take you home."

She nodded, wishing he'd wrap her in his arms. Kiss her. Tell her they could go back to the way things were before he'd broken her heart and told her they weren't meant to be together.

"Have you seen the paper today?" He pointed toward the copy on the small table in the interview room as she gathered her things to head home.

"I saw you must have sent out a press release about your experience with the Destroyers as a kid." The article had been short, but Kyle had told her they were eager to publicize Axel's version of his past before the news leaked about Jaako's arrest and attempted blackmail. "I thought it was well-handled."

Her cell phone chimed and she turned it off, not wanting to disrupt their conversation.

"The Murphys have great connections." They walked out of the interview room, and he gestured toward the front entrance, holding doors for her on their way out. "Kyle had everything ready for me to make a formal announcement last night. I think it was his way of apologizing for letting you out of his sight at the viewing party."

In the parking lot, he pointed to the car his brother

had left for them, a midnight-blue Audi Coupe in keeping with the showroom vehicles his family seemed to favor.

"He really didn't have a chance to keep me there since I sneaked out right behind you."

"You're too impulsive," he muttered, but there wasn't much heat in the words. He opened the car door for her but she didn't get inside.

She put her hands on her hips, bracing herself to stand up to this strong-willed man whom she desperately wanted in her life.

"Maybe *you're* too stubborn, or you would have let me help you come up with a better plan in the first place."

Sheltered from the station's view by a police van, Axel reached for her as they stood toe to toe. He sketched a touch along her jaw that melted her insides even though she wasn't nearly done giving him a piece of her mind.

"Don't you get it?" He spoke to her tenderly, his words as soft as his touch. "I needed to protect you. I nearly had a heart attack when you showed up there last night."

"I didn't think they'd catch me," she admitted, knowing she'd messed up. "But if I had to do it all over again…" She shrugged. "I don't know what I would do differently."

"You realize how much that scares the hell out of me?" His blue eyes warmed to a darker shade and she wished she could stare into them forever.

"So don't get into trouble anymore," she ventured, bringing up the idea of a future. "And I won't have to bail you out."

His fingers hesitated where he touched her.

"I've got a better idea." His squared jaw warned her he would be digging his heels in on this point.

"Try me." She wanted to turn her cheek toward his hand and place a kiss in his palm. Actually, she'd be content to kiss him anywhere.

"How about you stay with me and then neither of us will get into trouble without the other?" He stroked his fingers through her hair, combing gently. Slowly.

"Stay…with you?" she repeated, wanting to be sure she got this right.

A car backed out of a spot near them, but they ignored it, wrapped up in the moment.

"Yes." He twined a lock of hair around his finger, his gaze probing hers. "You could find social causes to film in Philadelphia as easily as you can in New York. And if you decide to traipse through gang terrain or get on the wrong side of some corrupt government official, I'll be there to make sure no one hassles you."

Pleasure sparked, a warm hopefulness that lit her up from within.

"My own personal defenseman." She pretended to mull that over, knowing she wasn't going anywhere if Axel Rankin wanted her to stay. "You could help keep me safe while I fix the problems in the world, one film at a time."

"It seems like fitting penance for a former gang member." He was only half joking, she knew.

No matter that he'd only been a kid at the time, Axel carried guilt in his heart from those days in Helsinki. He didn't know it, but healing that guilt was going to be one of her secret causes. He was too good of a man to be weighed down by those dark days.

"No." Shaking her head, she stepped closer, needing to feel that connection between them after how scared she'd been for him the night before. "It seems like fitting penance for telling me we didn't belong together."

A police car peeled out of the station with the siren on, the sound piercing at such near distance, but that didn't begin to faze her after what she and Axel had gone through last night.

"I didn't mean that," he admitted, folding his arms around her waist and pulling her close. "Although you can't deny you've had reservations about my lifestyle."

Awareness simmered in her blood and she breathed in his scent. She wondered how much room there was in the backseat of an Audi.

"For a so-called hockey goon, you sure are good at reading people."

"I'm only good at reading you." He placed a kiss at her temple, a soft slide of his lips along her hairline. "That's because I can't ever take my eyes off you."

"Well, I think we can work around our lifestyles, don't you?" She would never be a trophy wife with a standing spa appointment or a home on the cover of design magazines. "I could probably be swayed by the benefits of a bigger house and maybe you'd see the light and buy a hybrid."

His laughter rumbled through his chest and warmed hers. She looped her arms around his neck, knowing she'd never let him go.

"Sounds like you've already got a plan."

"Just ask anyone who knows me. I'm a problem solver."

"Speaking of which, do you think your sister would be interested in trying on a Philadelphia school for size?"

The question stopped her. Made her heart trip up its rhythm.

"Honestly?" She wasn't sure her sister would agree, but the fact that he'd offered...wow.

"I like big families." The certainty in his voice told her they were going to agree on the important things in life. The things that really mattered. "And no one knows better than me that you don't have to be born into a family to feel that connection."

Tears warmed her eyes unexpectedly and she was grateful for the cool spring breeze that helped her keep them at bay. Even if she couldn't convince her sister to come for school, she could picture Julia staying with them for the summers.

"Thank you," she whispered, choked up and ready to fall into that fancy car with him. Cover him with kisses.

"Anything for you." He captured her lips and she felt her knees turn to jelly.

She wanted nothing more than to lose herself in that

kiss, to dream of forever with her sexy hockey player, the stubborn Finn who was more than a match for her.

But an abrupt honk from a nearby car interrupted the sweet heat flowing in her veins.

"Jen? Axel?" Bryce the cameraman shouted at them through the rolled-down window of a white Ford rental sedan, his voice an unexpected intrusion. "Sorry to startle you. You must have your phones turned off."

"With good reason, dude. We're kind of busy here." Axel tucked her closer. "What's up?"

Bryce grinned. "A lady from the features page is at the practice rink. Stacy someone or other. She wants to do a special about how Ax's life turned around after the gang years. Colin thought it would be good to jump on this to boost the ratings—"

"Not right now." Jennifer didn't want to share Axel, no matter how good the publicity might be. They'd have time enough to make sure he talked to at-risk teens in the area. Told his story in places that might save other kids from making the same mistakes. For now, she needed him.

"Are you sure?" Bryce pressed. "You know how Colin is."

But Jennifer was done kowtowing to her boss for the chance to make the stories she wanted. The good ratings on the hockey documentary were going to be her ticket to a stronger voice in the production company. And if he wouldn't listen? She had options now. Commercial credentials.

"Colin will survive. You can tell the reporter—

Stacy—she'll just have to watch the next installment of the documentary," Jennifer told him while Axel waved the guy's car away.

Alone again, she sealed her aching body to the hard strength of Axel's, ready to go home. She closed her eyes as he dropped a kiss on the juncture of her neck and her shoulder, the warm puff of his breath making her skin tingle everywhere at once.

Edging away from her heated flesh, Axel grinned.

"He could have just told her that I get one hell of a happy ending," he added, right before he backed Jennifer into the car and reminded her why they were meant to be together after all.

* * * * *